PENGUIN BOOKS

Lime|Bar

Matt Condon was born in Queensland and has lived in the UK, Germany and France. His first work of fiction, *The Motorcycle Cafe*, was published in 1988. *Lime Bar* is his seventh fictional work for adults, and follows the highly acclaimed novel *The Pillow Fight*, published in 1998. He has also written a children's book, *The Tunnel* (1997). Matt Condon's novels have been shortlisted for several literary prizes, and his collections of short fiction have won two Steele Rudd awards. He currently lives in Sydney.

D1233641

MATT CONDON

Lime|Bar

PENGUIN BOOKS

Parts of this novel appeared in an earlier form in the *Adelaide Review*.

Penguin Books Australia Ltd
487 Maroondah Highway, PO Box 257
Ringwood, Victoria 3134, Australia
Penguin Books Ltd
Harmondsworth, Middlesex, England
Penguin Putnam Inc.
375 Hudson Street, New York, New York 10014, USA
Penguin Books Canada Limited
10 Alcorn Avenue, Toronto, Ontario, Canada M4V 3B2
Penguin Books (NZ) Ltd
Cnr Rosedale and Airborne Roads, Albany, Auckland, New Zealand
Penguin Books (South Africa) (Pty) Ltd
24 Sturdee Avenue, Rosebank, Johannesburg 2196, South Africa
Penguin Books India (P) Ltd
11, Community Centre, Panchsheel Park, New Delhi 110 017, India

First published by Penguin Books Australia Ltd 2001

1 3 5 7 9 10 8 6 4 2

Copyright © Matt Condon 2001

Designed by David Altheim, Penguin Design Studio
Cover photography by Getty Images
Typeset in 11/15.5 Charter by Post Pre-press Group, Brisbane
Printed and bound in Australia by McPherson's Printing Group
Maryborough, Victoria

National Library of Australia
Cataloguing-in-Publication data:

Condon, Matt (Matthew Steven), 1962– .

Lime Bar.

ISBN 0 14 100085 6.

1. Interpersonal relations – Fiction. I. Title.

A823.3

www.penguin.com.au

FOR GRANT JONES

ONE

Acres of Flutes

OFTEN, before they have even left the bar, the veil of their perfume trailing towards the door, I will tap a finger for Gustave to deliver the two perfect halves of a lime to me.

'Thank you, Gustave,' I say.

'Of course,' he replies quietly, briefly closing his eyes. He slowly passes me the silver dish of lime halves, as if it were the ashes urn of a dead relative.

I will, for a moment, study the halves: the symmetry of their moist segments, the thinness of the skin. I may select one half and examine it more closely. Or absently turn it about with my fingertips.

Gustave will then place before me a thick tumbler half-filled with ice and gin, and a small bottle of tonic water. At my leisure, I will gently squeeze one of the lime halves over the ice and watch the juice fuse with the gin. I may stay in the bar only for the duration of the single lime, and the amount of juice it yields. I have been known to remain for six limes, although eleven and a half limes is my record.

(Gustave occasionally refers to *that* evening as 'the ravaging of the orchard'. He can, at times, be a horticultural wit.)

Tonight feels, to me, like a three-lime evening.

'*Non*?' Gustave asks politely, gesturing towards the door of the bar, and the woman who has left me.

'No,' I say.

'Next time.'

'Yes. Next time.'

I wonder, pinching the soft leather of the lime skin I hold above my tumbler, if I know any longer what I am looking for in life. They come to my favourite spot at the end of the long, silver-topped bar to meet me. I stand, smiling, and greet them warmly. I compliment them on their hair, clothes, perfume. I guide them onto a stool and ask them their drink of preference.

We talk and they tell me about themselves, and I listen attentively (I am told by Gustave that this is one of the keys to *femme procurer*), and still, no matter how attractive they are, and interesting, I find myself disappearing from the moment. I leach away, just as the lime juice is enveloped by the gin. And our rendezvous, not unlike the squeezed lime half, will lose body, and shape, and it is over.

I am resisting the urge to say, sentimentally, that I sit in these empty moments like the fleshy, ragged pulp exposed in the half-bladder of used lime – but that is how I feel.

'Another please, Gustave,' I say, and my second lime is delivered.

How long has this been going on? I can tell you exactly. The latest, Bernice, who is now probably well across the

Harbour Bridge in the back of a taxi, was the eleventh woman in almost eighteen months. I reach over and touch the top of her stool, hoping for a residue of warmth.

'A slump,' says Gustave, reassuringly.

'You think so?'

'It happens to us all, *monsieur*. It is the way of the men and the women. At times it can resemble – how do you say? – the machine of the pinball.'

'I see,' I say.

'We are collisions, *monsieur*.'

'Of course.'

I wonder, too, if I have not become some sort of oddity here, in the Lime Bar.

It has not always been the Lime Bar. I adopted it as my regular while it was still the Slipyard Hotel, a dark cavern filled with the shadows of seafaring types, or men who fancied they were related to the sea. Its sandstone walls were draped with lengths of thick rope and wooden imitation ships' wheels, and behind the bar were two battered, jade-green pearling divers' helmets. How often I had sat at the bar and wondered about the pearl divers who had once donned those helmets. Men lowered to the bottom of the ocean, their world viewed through the narrowest of portholes, their excitement steaming up the thick glass. Lumbering slowly and clumsily in search of those perfect white spheres that would one day rest gently against the powdered skin and collarbone dip of a woman. The pearls all men seek, peering hopefully through their foggy helmet glass, inching through weed and coral and the vastness of the ocean.

Then they sold the Slipyard Hotel and within weeks the new owners had it shelled, so that when the doors reopened there was nothing left of the salty shadows and blue-braided hats and dogs snoring under stools. Instead, it was all pale timbers and stainless-steel surfaces and glass. Some of the regulars kept attending, pulling up designer bar stools in the approximate region of where they had drunk for years, for decades, in the Slipyard. (How sad it was to see them perched unsteadily on the high stools, looking down and checking the legs, alone in an unfamiliar crow's nest.) They were faithful to their geography, as most men tend to be. But the new world of the Lime Bar buffeted them about and, eventually, beached them elsewhere.

I have considered moving on, to a different meeting place. But I am fond of Gustave. He is the only legitimate Frenchman I know. I have often asked him, 'Gustave, are you a legitimate Frenchman?' And he answers, '*Oui.*' He is slim and has the deep, almost greenish, permanent five o'clock shadow of the legitimate Frenchman, and he wears his coal-black hair oiled back off the forehead. I have no idea why he is here at the bottom of the world and not in France where he is totally legitimate. Perhaps he is here for reasons of the illegitimate. I don't wish to know.

As for the Lime Bar, there is no other place that would respect the lime the way its barman Gustave respects the lime. The quality of the limes here is consistent and unmatched. I have personally met Gustave's supplier – a small and neat Asian grower with an unparalleled knowledge of his citrus – and this, too, is comforting. I have only to inspect the actual lime trees to complete the chain of knowledge, to trace to its source what is now one of my only pleasures. And Gustave has promised me a trip to the lime orchard some weekend, perchance with one of his famous French picnic hampers.

'A fresh coaster?' asks Gustave.

'*Merci*,' I say. This slipping into French I also like. How easily one can become cosmopolitan after several of Gustave's gins.

I admire the illustration of a lime on the surface of the new coaster. As I have done many times in the past year and a half, I flip the coaster over, having first ensured the surface of the bar is dry, and as always jot a few notes on the thick white cardboard. I find, by the arrival of my third lime, that the theories come quickly. Sometimes they arrive so fast I can barely catch up to them with my small, cramped handwriting.

'Another?' asks Gustave.

'Please.'

And I continue – a word here, a phrase there – until the gin and lime juice is no longer carrying me along, but has apprehended me, and I slip the coasters into my coat pocket.

This is the dangerous time. I have considered, more than once, that I am having a nervous breakdown. I have weighed up the possibility that I will remain alone for the rest of my life. That the quest has no purpose. And I am astounded that now, at 45, I have only just begun to look for patterns in my life. Why does the search for meaning always seem to start too late?

'*Monsieur*?' Gustave asks.

He stands there, behind the bar, with a perfect lime in his open palm.

'Sure,' I say, inspecting the specimen. 'No, I'm sorry: *mais oui*, Gustave, and *merci beaucoup*.'

I watch as he carefully bisects the lime with the blade of a large, stainless-steel knife.

The halves fall apart, as if in slow motion, rock briefly, then are still, side by side, on the chopping block.

'For *monsieur* it is on the house,' says Gustave, placing them before me on the silver dish and topping up my ice and gin.

I nod in gratitude. I think that the relationship I have with Gustave may be the only appropriate type. He asks for no explanations. He has never queried my taking of notes on the back of the Lime Bar's coasters, or their contents. He knows instinctively when to offer solace, or congratulation. He keeps the silver-topped bar without blemish. And I never need to tell him what I want.

I wonder why this silent arrangement cannot be recreated with other human beings. I think of all the preamble, the false compliments, the laboured conversations I have had here, at my place at the bar, with good, decent women. The rolls and rolls of barbed wire laid out between each other. The crawling on the belly. The snipping with pliers. The cuts and tears we suffer on the way. And for what? There is no barbed wire between Gustave and me. Just the clean silver top of the bar, and the glint of his perfect knife.

I see, at the other end of the room, a young couple I met a fortnight ago. On that night I had said hello to Lauren but our conversational tank had, after just one hour, run out of gas, and so I had started talking to them. I still had chatter in me, but not for Lauren. I had shouted them drinks. Several, in fact. The boy – his name escapes me, but I have it written down on a coaster, somewhere – had admired my American money clip. The conversation went there, to the money clip. It followed the clip for a while, then moved on, to my business, and on, after more drinks, to my break-up with Margaret, and deeper, much deeper than I had intended and, from the expressions on their faces, than they had expected also. This is how it is, in this period. It takes nothing more than a solid silver American money clip, with its flat, embedded rhinestone near the hinge, to channel directly into the vast reserve of personal trauma that sits like a dark well of artesian water inside me, giving off its strange noises, eddying and rocking to its own rhythm. The girl, I remember, had pinched the boy's arm, and they left in a courteous manner. I look down the long bar to them now, where they sit with their backs to me.

'You have to get back in the saddle,' says my squash companion Neil.

But Neil can say this, casually, as he adjusts his squash goggles. Because Neil does not have to concern himself with saddles, and new wardrobes of clothes (not too young for your age, but not your age either), and blind dates, and dinner parties wholly constructed around you and a stranger, and meetings that are the result of long, entangled and mostly tenuous connections – my mother has a girlfriend whose sister, et cetera – and intended to bring together two people out of all the people in the world. Neil just has to go home to his family. Neil has never ridden a horse in his life.

It is the 'down the barrel' factor that I hate. I have jotted my theories about 'down the barrel' on some early coasters. I have, at some point, crossed the line for any hope of a future. I am looking 'down the barrel'. I once used this phrase quite liberally, as a young businessman, when I had all the time in the world to play with. And suddenly I am inside the cliché itself. I am the tiny, helmeted figure clinging to the lip of the cannon, waiting for someone – I know not whom – to light the fuse and fire me across the universe.

Gustave has never used the phrase 'down the barrel' in relation to me.

I tap my finger for a fourth lime. It is a superfluous gesture between us. Gustave hesitates, momentarily, then proceeds with the ritual. It is not rude, this tapping. It is something I have learned in my business dealings with the Chinese. It is a long tale, about an emperor and his servant. I shan't go into it. But it is, may I add, a supreme sign of respect, a sort of bowing with the fingers, and Gustave – French as he is – is aware of this. But four limes could lead to five. Then six.

The bar is filling with drinkers who have spilled out of other hotels. It is here they come for a 'roadie', or to finish business unfinished in other establishments, or to start business that may not have got off the ground earlier in the evening. There is much business done here.

All this is, after my many years of marriage to Margaret, a new experience for me. It is a completely different terrain from the business lunch, where I once frolicked as a married man. And different again from my earlier days at the local tennis club, where I met Margaret. And it is the surface of the moon compared with the many fine cocktail parties and soirées I attended, Margaret on my arm, during the peak years of my wheelings and dealings, which ultimately led me briefly into the heart of State Parliament, where I once bought the Premier a brandy. But I was a mere dragonfly there, my feet brushing the lily pad of power.

'You are certain, *monsieur*?'

I again tap the bar gently. Gustave smiles cautiously. He looks me in the eye as he slices the lime, trying to work out if I am to go for my record. He has lifted an eyebrow ever so slightly. I ignore the eyebrow.

I have told my women nothing about me, because by the time they have stopped talking about themselves and it is my turn – 'So what about you?' – I find myself so loathsome that I cannot continue. There is no talk of my youthful interest in yachting. Nor is there discussion of my cigars in the humidor of my cigar dealer in the city. I am at an age where any such dialogue can be construed as big-noting. Where just a breathy reference to a humidor could send them away.

Maybe it is the gin. Or the brief memory of Bernice on the stool beside me. But everything is so fragile. Everything, between men and women. The whole floor of it is acres of upturned crystal champagne flutes. I was never prepared for this.

I am halfway through writing this down – about the champagne flutes – when I am tapped lightly myself, on the shoulder. I look up at Gustave, surprised. He is wiping more glasses. He has caught the tap on my shoulder in the bar mirror. His head turns quickly. I turn, too, and face a young woman with long auburn hair and deep red lips and a small, dark mole on the precipice of her left cheekbone.

'Excuse me,' she says. 'Could I have a light?'

I am stunned for some seconds. I cannot make sense of her sentence. I feel the cold of the silver-topped bar beneath my right palm. I stare at the island of the mole.

'I'm sorry?'

'I was wondering if you had a light.'

The two halves of the new lime sit near me on the bar. I can see them out of the corner of my right eye. Then, unexpectedly, a white square of light enters my peripheral vision. A little opening in the great, heavy expanse of silver. I turn to it, and discover it is a matchbook. I have never seen this matchbook. I don't ordinarily smoke. Only cigars, from the humidor, and they are several kilometres away, cosy and comfortable and sleeping next to each other in their timber bed.

'Of course,' I say.

I open the matchbook with its miniature lime on the cover, and see Gustave looking at me briefly in the mirror before he leaves us.

I light a match, and the vivid green head is consumed by white, then yellow flame, and I hold it, trembling, towards the woman. She leans forward, and as she draws in, the very breath of her, from inside her, pulling the flame towards the tiny cylinder of tobacco, I look up, and she is staring at me, and we are held there, joined, for a second, with fire connected to the match connected to my fingertips, and her breath, her lungs, pulling me to her, and there is light in our eyes.

I do not even blow out the match.

'A drink?' I ask, standing.

And still holding the burning black stem of the match, which is, interestingly, curling itself over to form the beginnings of a question mark, I lead her by the elbow onto the stool, the dying flame a lantern. The flame goes out, and I barely feel the burn at my fingertips.

The Emperor of Goat
Island

GUSTAVE has often forewarned that during this time of being 'between love' I will become obsessed with my reflection.

'It is not the narcissus, *monsieur*. It is the need to verify that you still exist. You see,' Gustave points to my fractured reflection in the back mirror of the Lime Bar, bits of my head and upper torso obscured by bottles of spirits, my visage sometimes passing through the empty portions of the bottles, 'this is you. The jigsaw of the booze, *monsieur*,' he says, pleased with the observation.

I thank him. Of all the races I have encountered in the world, I have found the French the most accidentally existential.

Now, sitting here in the wide alcove of the window in Room 417 of the Stork Hotel, at 5.37 a.m., attached to a bitter cigar, I look at the shadowed relief of my face in the glass. As I draw on the cigar, the glowing tip sketches me in amber. Good. Despite the frightful realisation that I am getting old – or can I blame the inferior quality of the cigar light? – I at least appear to exist.

Larissa, my new friend from the Lime Bar, is snoring lightly in the bedroom behind me. It is a beautiful thing to hear a young woman snoring. A few hours earlier I had gone quietly to her side of the bed and simply watched her sleeping, a tangle of auburn hair across her cheek. Her breath smelled of sour coffee. It was not unpleasant. But even that – taking in a woman's breath – had reminded me of Margaret. And it was not just her gentle breath, or the shape of her sleeping on her side in this hotel bed, but the room itself that seemed so familiar to me – the botanically accurate prints of pine cones and leaves, the sofa, the armchairs, the deep window alcove. This had been Margaret's and my favourite hotel in the city. It was to the Stork that we 'went away' for weekends, to disappear from the world.

As I look out to the harbour I see the small, dark shape that is Goat Island. There are a few fading pinpoints of light scattered across it. A wharf. And a red beacon, not unlike the tip of this cheap cigar.

That was our island, too. Margaret's and mine.

It was there, on the island, that I first made love to Margaret all those years ago. I remember we had played tennis at Birchgrove that morning. It was how I met women then, in the early days.

'You will find a wife, always, on the courts,' my father had once mused, tossing this pearl to me from his study no doubt, or from the rich leather interior of his Jaguar as he departed for some meeting or luncheon or dinner appointment – it was, from memory, one of the few times he ever said anything remotely personal to me.

So Margaret and I, only acquaintances to each other, although known, always known, as a part of crowds that, week after week, intersected and touched rims and, sometimes, clashed stupendously – at the races, the balls, the polo – played tennis at Birchgrove and then picnicked on Goat Island.

We, the males, the stags, of the crowds had always been trying to outdo each other. Our courting became competitive. Dates would take the form of a seaplane ride over the city, a spin in a sports car on a racing track out of town, a chartered flight interstate simply for a night at the theatre.

My friend Oliver once hired Australia's top-seeded female tennis player to give his girlfriend, Heidi, four hours of personal lessons. Heidi had suffered a slump in her mid-week competition, and the seed had brought her back to form. Oliver and Heidi became engaged three weeks later. They now have two children. Neither of them plays tennis any longer. The seeded player made it to the fourth round of Wimbledon, then retired. She never even wrote a memoir.

The Goat Island picnic with Margaret was not extravagant. It involved nothing more than a water taxi, a gourmet hamper and a shaded spot beneath the trees.

The food was fine. We talked of tennis, naturally, and the crowds, and our plans, for we of the crowds always had plans. There was always something urgent to be done in the future, something ahead that held greater importance than the moment we were actually living. We of the crowds were constantly chasing something, although none of us ever glimpsed it, save for some wobbling and indistinct chimera that hovered not a kilometre off the port side of our yachts, or beyond the pall of our cigar smoke, or in the hills behind the golf course, teasing us through the blue gums.

But Margaret. Perhaps it was the stimulation of the morning's tennis, or the champagne, or the heat of that summer day. We went from having never touched each other to full, satisfying and, might I say, somewhat animalistic sex on a tartan rug. And I had one of the strangest moments of my life at that instant, gripping Margaret's perfect buttocks. I imagined that the animals at Taronga Zoo, across the harbour, were watching us fornicate. I saw in my mind the querulous looks of giraffe and zebra, of elephant and chimpanzee. I felt not only emperor of Goat Island, but of all the beasts.

'You beast,' she had whispered.

'Thank you so much,' I replied, all puffed and primed with that ludicrous flush of masculinity.

When we finished, we just resumed our luncheon, as if the lovemaking had been a thread in the rich design of our excursion – champagne, olives, chicken, sex, coffee from a Thermos – and it was assumed, from that moment, that we were 'together'.

I look at Goat Island now – the heat from the tip of this cheap cigar already burning my lips, although I am only half-finished – and it seems to sit heavy in the water of the harbour. A leaden mole of rock and foliage, immovable, and there to remind me of the life I once had. Sometimes I wake and peer bleary eyed through the sliding glass doors of my tiny bachelor flat, hoping it has drifted out to sea during the night and disappeared. It is the terrible thing about memories. We are nothing without them – Isn't that all we are, Gustave? Vessels for memory? – yet with them they can make us nothing.

Larissa murmurs. I turn to see her changing position in the bed, and then the sweet snoring resumes. What is her head full of now? Boys and butterflies? Restaurant lamps and stars? What do I know?

When we arrived at the hotel after midnight, I recognised the concierge and he winked before tipping the brim of his hat. I had felt ashamed, somewhat dirty, when I had first brought them here and been recognised by the staff. I was almost used to it now. But places hold a residue of our lives, and I need only glimpse the familiar shape of a stork pressed into the ashtray sand, or disappear into the mahogany-panelled lift, to feel the presence of Margaret. Her fingerprints are still in this hotel.

In these strange times I usually secure a room with a view of Goat Island, and I usually go through the marble tub routine, and the foreplay in the glow of the city through the giant hotel window panes (for, with men of my age, direct artificial light is to be avoided), and the retreat to the window alcove. My new track. Through the forest.

Larissa seems to be laughing in her sleep. The sky is getting lighter and Goat Island is taking shape. I think I can see the trees under which Margaret and I made love that day. How torrid it was. Had we sent the Taronga animals into a frenzy?

I stub out the cigar and the crackling of the tobacco, the collapse of the loose leaf, seems very loud in the hotel room.

I look over, then, to Balmain peninsula, and I can make out the block of flats where I live. I inspect the cube of red brick and think I can identify my lounge-room windows. I expect, funnily, to see myself at the sliding doors, looking at Goat Island from a different angle. (It is, of course, Gustave's reflection theory. How infuriatingly insightful he can be at times.) Is that really me? A slight paunch, although not bad for my age. The raffish curls tipped with grey, the eyes – as I've been told by my many female friends at the Lime Bar – of a mischievous child? That's me? So depressingly indistinguishable from everyone else?

I would have taken Larissa, and all the others, to the flat after our meeting in the Lime Bar, but it has the ambience of an airport terminal. It exists, in my bachelorhood, simply as a sort of tree house, with 'PRIVATE – KEEP OUT' nailed to the door. I don't know how this has happened.

My squash partner Neil tells me it is entirely natural.

'You are a child again,' he says.

'Thank you, Neil.'

'You're back at the start. You've got to learn to walk once more.'

'I appreciate your support.'

'It's a whole different world for you now. There are people who have someone, and people who don't, and they're like different planets.'

'Please continue. I'm feeling better already.'

'Hey, I know what it's like. I left Mardi for six weeks once – you remember – and it was, well, it was hell.'

'My condolences.'

'It was the shopping I couldn't stand. It was buying the *vegetables*, in the *vegetable* department. That did it for me. I knew I couldn't be alone. I'm not an alone person. I'm a people's person.'

'Definitely not a *vegetable* person.'

'You see? You've become cynical as well. That'll happen to you. When you're on your own. Whose serve is it, anyway?'

And he's partially right, of course. I hate it when Neil is even partially right. I doubt he has ever been in a vegetable department in his life. He is a shop-on-the-Internet sort of guy. One of those painfully technologically literate men who fill their conversations with software and computer brand numbers and words that only begin with 'e'. I think he is an e-pain in the e-arse, but I don't tell him. He is one of the few remaining links to my old life. And that link, if the truth be known, is nothing more substantial than the blurred trajectory of a squash ball.

I took the flat, after Margaret and I separated, without any consideration for what it might entail. I think I expected to come home to it on the first night and toss the car keys on the hallway table, as I had always done, and pour myself a brandy and sit in my favourite chair and read the *New Yorker* and wait for dinner to be served. As I had always done.

But I did not have a hall, let alone a hallway table. I had for a chair a vinyl bean bag that mysteriously excreted its foam-ball innards, whenever it chose, from some unfindable orifice, and I had lost my passion for reading anything but foodstuff labels.

I had walked into the flat, on that inaugural night, to nothing. Just the lights of the city through the sliding doors, the scuttle of cockroaches in the kitchen, the muted sound of laughter from somewhere – above, next door, below – and my view of Goat Island.

I took the next morning off and purchased saucepans and cutlery and domestic cleaning items. I bought a rubber bath mat and soaps and shampoo. I filled a trolley with frozen foods and dried apricots. Then I took them all back to the flat and put them where I thought they should be put, and it did not make any difference. There are few things sadder than the sight of a jar of dried apricots in a bachelor flat.

So it is that I take this room, or one very much like it, in the Stork. I know the hotel porters and the receptionists better than I do the people in the adjoining flats. Another thin life has opened for me, different from the one that presented itself when I left Margaret, but parallel. I wonder how many more await me. How many more doors I have to go through.

The sun is up. Larissa is still sleeping soundly. She has flicked back the covers, and I see her young breasts. She is younger than Margaret was when we first spread out the tartan rug under the trees on Goat Island. I briefly check to see if the island is still there, and notice that my reflection has completely disappeared.

I know I won't see Larissa again. I know she will be disappointed at how I was unable to give her pleasure. She may at least take away a humorous story, to share with her girlfriends, from this room in the Stork Hotel. Maybe she will go about her business, driving to or from work or to a restaurant or a nightclub, and from somewhere in the city she will catch sight of the neon stork on top of the building, and she will laugh.

I dress quietly. I leave the room and settle the account at reception. I take a cab back over the Anzac Bridge and see, out of the corner of my eye, beyond the container terminals, the shape of Goat Island.

I stand at the sliding glass doors of my flat and look out to the city and see the Stork Hotel. I count the floors and find the window of what I think is my room, where Larissa is probably still sleeping.

All I can see, in my mind, is a collapsed cylinder of dry tobacco leaf amongst small, fragile rolls of ash.

THREE

Heir to the Golf Locker

MY father first told me about sex on the eighteenth hole of the Australian Golf Club course.

Now that I am as old as he was when he spoke to me about carnality on that day, it does not surprise me that he chose the course, with its pretty, flowered walkway to the eighteenth – the most dangerous par five that the game could summon – to impart a lesson in life.

I was twelve. It was my first father-and-son round of golf. He had deemed me of an age to be introduced to this other world he had, this other country – the Australian Golf Club. And, it seemed, old enough to know about sex.

'You have a penis,' he said, shockingly, removing a kangaroo-skin cover from his one wood. He had, only seconds before, been instructing me on the hole's infamous water hazards. And then had come the rush of genitals.

'And the woman, she has a vagina,' he added, cleaning the head of his club with a towel. 'Are you listening to me, boy?'

'Yes, sir.'

He teed up.

'The penis,' he said curtly, 'goes into the vagina. Are we clear?'

'Yes.'

'Good,' he said, stepping back from the ball and surveying the long carpeted expanse of the fairway. He swung, then, and struck the ball cleanly. He followed its trajectory.

'And don't go playing with yourself,' he added, almost as an aside. 'It's not healthy.'

I was unsure, still sitting in the small electric cart, if he was referring to golf or to sexual matters. I did not dare question him.

Later, after the round, I waited in my father's car while he shared drinks with some of his friends at the club's all-male locker-room bar. I thought of what he had told me on the eighteenth tee but made little sense of it. I knew, some-how, we had shared something that would remain between us, that would never again be mentioned, and that would always belong to the gardenias and honeysuckle of the final hole.

The moment would, years later, crystallise, and I would forever associate sex with my father's tartan trousers and white golf shirt, with his 210-metre drive to the right of that fairway, and with his tee – an orange plastic naked woman holding up the small dish that cradled the ball.

Funnily, in the thirty-odd years since that day, I have never parred the eighteenth.

I had not expected then that I would still be playing golf

with my father all these years later, and that in the time of my impending divorcehood he would again choose to become intimate with me about sex. When I was married there was never a word mentioned. But now that I have almost come through 'the marriage thing', as he puts it, this seems to have broken a seal within him. Suddenly he feels free to tell lewd jokes, and even discuss his own periodic philanderings. I begin to realise, round after round, that I have never known him.

It is Saturday morning. I am to meet him in the clubhouse at 10.30 a.m. for an 11.07 a.m. tee off. As I drive to the course I flush with embarrassment at the memory of the night before, with Larissa in the Stork. We are never, no matter what age, beyond the grip of embarrassment.

When I arrive at the clubhouse he is not there. I proceed, as I always do, to the locker room.

I understand why my father spends so much time at the club, for the locker room is hardly what you would expect of a locker room. It is more like the large sitting room of a hunting lodge. The perfect hunting lodge of the imagination, with oiled guns at the door and game passing freely outside. A flow of game traffic that never diminishes so that men, tired of cribbage and malt whisky, with an ember of testosterone flaring to life, may simply step out the front door and fell a deer with a single shot.

There are leather couches here in the locker room, a fireplace, rugs. There is an adjacent bathroom with small, individual hand towels. There are showers and spas. There are complimentary dishes of crackers and cheese. If you leave your golf shoes tossed willy-nilly after a round, they are immaculately polished and returned, miraculously, to the foot of your locker.

The whole place is, I have finally understood, my father's own lodge in the mountains. It is his refuge from the world. There are no women.

After that first round with him when I was 12, I automatically became a junior club member. This is expected of the sons of men like my father. This is a birthright.

And from that moment, too, I was given the privilege of sharing his private locker. Number 371.

'Here,' he said to me on the day of the sex talk, when he finally emerged from the bar. 'This is yours.'

He tossed me a key to the locker. I kept it on a special key ring. I knew, in the way that the boys of rich fathers know, that this was something precious and not to be taken for granted. I understood this because my father did not treat the moment as something precious. He was the same with his money. And my mother. That is how I knew it was important.

Since then, and over many years, I have shared my father's locker.

You have to see the banks of wooden lockers to appreciate what this means to me at this delicate stage in my life. They stand, row after row, with their small, engraved golden plates on the door, like the walls of the dead in a crematorium garden.

And this is how I view them now, having lost Margaret and being without love. I see my father's name on the plaque of our locker and then, when he is gone, a new plaque bearing my name, and then, after me, nothing. I am where the lineage of the locker will end. It has not helped my game, this midlife morbidity.

On this Saturday I open the locker and there, in the dark space that smells of damp grass, I see the bits and pieces that make up my father.

At the back there is a half-empty bottle of Irish whiskey. There is a pair of gleaming golf shoes. There is a floppy golfing hat, and a clutch of balls and tees, and a couple of cheap detective novels, a toiletries bag, an asthma inhaler, and numerous pairs of crushed trousers and shorts. There are also three bottles of tablets for my father's heart.

I occupy very little space in the locker. I may keep a wet-weather jacket there, an umbrella, a clean pair of socks. But not a lot else. I look in that locker and I know it is us – my father takes up the bulk of the space still, in his mid-seventies, and I, always the 12-year-old, remain quietly in a corner.

I sit before the giant stone fireplace, above which is a large watercolour of ancient golfers in their plus-fours, and wait for him. It is what I have always done – sat and waited, in the foyer of his office, outside his study at home, in the car at the front of a restaurant. Waited.

He arrives blustering, and larger than life, although he swears he has lost a couple of centimetres in height as he has aged. It is his booming voice that makes him bigger and taller than he is. In the old measurement, my father is five-nine, with a six-two voice. It carries from the foyer of the clubhouse.

He breezes past me and heads for the locker.

'You're early,' he says, rather than admitting he is late.

Within minutes his personal cart, laden with our clubs, has been brought out on the driveway downstairs. He takes the wheel.

There is little reason to talk. We have done this so many times. He lights his traditional first-tee cigar and clips it into a specially made holder in the centre of the cart's steering wheel. We tee off on the first.

There are many types of golfers. There are golfers who take a long time preparing for the shot. They may practise their swing three or four times before hitting. They will look ahead, after each swing, imagining the passage of the ball. These types of golfers play two games simultaneously – the imagined round and the real round.

And there are those who waste no time. Who make no practice swings, and hit quickly. It is these golfers who, after the shot, remain frozen in the post-swing position, as still as statues, waiting to see what fate has delivered them. This is how my father plays.

'Shit,' he says, as the ball skips into a bed of pine needles to the left of the fairway.

And then it's over. He never simmers over a misdirected shot. It is his way. I presume it is the basis of his success.

We continue on. We say little. My father's giant cigar continues to smoulder. It is the aroma of the tobacco and the bouquet of freshly cut grass that I always associate with him.

'In the hole,' he urges himself, crouched over the ball with a pitching wedge. 'In the hole!'

I watch him with love and pity. It is the first time I have

thought about the possibility of my father ageing. Now, with the consciousness of my own ageing.

'You spoken to your mother recently?' he asks, puffing on the cigar.

'Last Sunday. We met for lunch.'

'Good.'

He tells me, later in the round, of his new personal assistant, and the dimensions of her breasts, and the length of her legs, and I think back to the night in the hotel room.

'They didn't make them like that in my day,' he says. 'But thank God they do now.'

I hate him talking like this. I see him step down into a giant, steep-walled bunker, and notice how small he is in this monstrous crater. How dwarfed.

'They've got these new Wonderbra things,' he continues. 'Have you seen them? The wonder of the Wonderbra.'

I wonder if men ever lose this. This sexual longing that the body ages around.

At the eighteenth he hops out of the cart and strides towards the tee. I realise this sacred place means nothing to him. It is as insignificant as his last putt, on the seventeenth. As I stand behind him, looking down that dangerous fairway, I think of Larissa in the hotel, and Margaret, and the blurred naked figures of my past – this long line of flesh and hair and cries that started here, on this spot, more than thirty years ago. And I realise he prepared me for nothing. That nobody can prepare anyone else for anything, ever. That we are all born fresh and new, and the chassis of us, well, the chassis has to take its own bumps and scratches along the way.

Back in the clubhouse, my father greets old friends and fills the room with his cannon-fire laugh.

He joins me at the bar, still talking, still shouting across the leather couches and low tables, and the barman asks, 'What will it be, Mr Wilson?'

And we both say, in unison, 'Bourbon and dry.'

He does not register the significance of the moment. He takes his drink and joins a group of friends.

I stand at the bar, a bourbon and dry in one hand, the other in the pocket of my golf trousers, fingering the key to locker 371. I look out at the greens and fairways and understand, at that moment, that I need to reconstruct my game completely. To break it all down and build it up from scratch. The swing, the technique, the mental approach. I have to dismantle myself.

'Gustave,' I declare, that evening in the Lime Bar. 'I must dismantle myself.'

'Pfffttt,' Gustave exclaims in his perfect French. 'Sounds very painful, *monsieur*.'

'Then make the next one a double,' I say.

'For the dismantling, *monsieur*, you may need more than that.'

I feel a cold wind whistling through me. In a single hinge action of the wrist, the drink is gone.

FOUR

Remembrance of Fists Past

MY father once told me never to hit anyone bigger than myself, or an Englishman.

'Why not Englishmen?' I asked.

'They fight dirty,' he said.

'In what way, dirty?'

'They use any which way to defeat you. Head butts, knees in the scrotum, biting your ears off, broken glasses in the neck, that's an Englishman for you.'

'Chair over the back of the head?'

'Chair over the back of the head.'

'I'm glad I'm not an Englishman,' I said.

'Be very glad, son.'

'What about the French?'

'They'll propose you meet at a later date. The next morning, say. On neutral territory. Then you'll turn up and they'll have a valet or a waiter arrive with a little note apologising that they've been delayed and asking could they arrange another meeting at a future time.'

'Americans?'

'They'll either talk you into submission first, or simply produce a gun and blow your head off.'

'Would they really? And Australians?'

'Knock your block off, then kiss you later and tell you they didn't mean it.'

'So I shouldn't fight Australians either?'

'Not unless you want to be kissed,' said my father.

I think of this, and a pupil named Sullivan from my old boys' school, as I stare at the envelope. It can't be. It isn't possible. Somehow they have caught up with me.

I handle the letter with great trepidation. The first alarming query is, how have they found me? How have they secured my postal address?

For starters, my postal address is unusual, and has, in the past, caused much alarm.

When I first applied for a post-office box, post-Margaret, I looked forward to its anonymity. Post-office boxes seem, to me, to say that you have established yourself. That an ordinary mailbox is insufficient. Post-office boxes are close to the source – the post office – which suggests that important documents and assorted mails have less distance to travel. They do not risk the hands of postmen. They are not carted around in post-office rucksacks and left to the unpredictabilities of the world.

So I approached the friendly folk in my local post office and asked for the largest post-office box they had. All three employees behind the counter looked at me darkly.

'I'm sorry,' said Basil, the post-office worker I have dealings with. 'We don't have any post-office boxes left.'

'None?'

'None.'

'But this is a post office. Post offices have to have boxes available, don't they?'

The other two employees, sensing my rising agitation, went into a whispered conference.

'Actually, we do have one, but you won't want it,' Basil said.

'What do you mean, I won't want it?'

'Nobody wants it. That's why it's the only one left.'

'What's wrong with it? What could be wrong with a post-office box?'

'You won't want it, sir.'

'It's me, Basil. Why are you calling me sir?'

'I'd advise against taking it.'

'It is a post-office box, is it not?'

'Yes.'

'And it's available?'

'Yes, it is.'

'Then I'll take it.'

The three looked at each other with concern.

'Very well,' said Basil.

And that was how I arrived at having the postal address of Box 666.

The devil's sign. The mailing address of Lucifer.

'Don't blame us if you go home and your house is burnt to the ground,' said Basil. (I like Basil. We have shared many humorous moments. Being a confirmed bachelor, as he always describes himself, he knows of my enforced bachelorhood and has tried to share the bonhomie of bachelors. As I am paying my meagre gas bill, he often exclaims, 'Who's the naughty boy who hasn't been eating at home, then?' There are enough codes in bachelorhood, I have discovered, to keep ASIO busy for several decades.)

But I had no problems with Box 666. I found it amusing that people could be so superstitious. I felt like trying to contact the owner of Box 69 to see if she or he had problems with perverts. I didn't think I would be getting strange letters from Satanists.

Still, here in my hand is a letter from those I have never expected to hear from again. Funny how the past sneaks up on you when you're looking for a future.

I open the letter slowly. Inside is a brief note, with a long list of names and addresses attached to it. It is signed by Peter Wolf, the chairman of the Xavier College Old Boys Committee.

Wolf. Wolf. I see his face hazily, his creamy skin and red hair not fully defined in my memory: a boy's face in the dim firelight of the past.

'We would be delighted,' the letter reads, 'if you could join your fellow classmates in a charity fundraiser for the impoverished children of Africa and informal reunion. The weekend will involve men's-only drinks on the Friday evening, and a cocktail party with wives or partners on the Saturday night. On Sunday, feel free to bring your children along to a reunion barbecue . . .'

Children along to a reunion barbecue? Cocktail parties with wives or partners? Peter Wolf, who defecated in the long-jump pit down on the school's main oval all those years ago? (Things are starting to come back in a rush.)

I study the list of names and addresses of Old Boys from my year who have been tracked down to date. I get halfway through the first page of names and have to pour myself a brandy.

Virtually all of them are there. Names I have not heard or read in years. Names that draw themselves out of a vast fog. Johnny Crank. James Smitts. Kevin O'Corcoran. Billie Judd. My God. Some of them are instantly recognisable. Who could forget school football jock Phil Hill? And Sam Pauls, the swimming champion they tipped to go on to the Olympics. Or the tennis champion Simon Little, a Wimbledon contender, or so the Jesuit Brothers told us. And my close boyhood pals, Ian Milton and Wayne Friars.

I can see their young faces. Faces that have remained frozen in time because I have never kept in touch with a single one of them.

Yet judging by their addresses a lot of them have remained close to their school companions and Xavier. All the sporting heroes, jocks and studs, bar the long-distance champion Paul Panozza (who had returned to his home village at the foot of Mt Etna), live within 10 kilometres of the old alma mater. A number of them in the same suburb. Grown men living near the old school after all these years, as if, in the mornings, it would give them no greater pleasure than to slip a packed lunch into their schoolbag and head off to class.

I put the letter down, pour a second brandy and stare at

the city skyline. What has happened, if anything, to these schoolmates since I last saw them in another life? What are they doing with themselves? Who amongst them have died? There are bound to have been deaths.

And what has happened to that boy Sullivan who inexplicably, one morning after parade, decided to smack me in the mouth, resulting in a chipped tooth and swollen lips? Where is Sullivan?

I am getting angry. I check the list again. Sure enough, there is his address. Incredible. It is only a few suburbs from here. Sullivan. It is Sullivan who makes the decision for me. Sullivan, who will now have to deal with the man whose address is the same as the devil's. We meet again, Sullivan.

The men's-only drinks is at a bar in the city. An hour before meeting time I am already dressed in my best suit and taking a few courage-building snifters at the Lime Bar.

'You are like the hot cat on the roof of tin,' says Gustave.

'I'm nervous,' I answer.

'Of a bunch of old men?' says Gustave, issuing his customary dismissive pfffttt.

'Thank you, Gustave. You are implying that I, too, am an old man?'

'You are too young to be an old man, but sometimes young men can be old.'

I remain puzzled by Gustave's cryptic musings.

'There is nothing sadder than the old young man, although the young old man can be even sadder,' he continues. 'Old young old man, that is what to aim for.'

'Old young old man?'

'Correct. It is a saying in France, that the old young old man has the greatest dignity and attitude to life.'

'I have never heard that said in France.'

'Then you must be deaf, *mon ami*, like an old man.'

'Can I be a young old young old man?'

'You are such a silly person,' he says, moving down the bar.

I arrive at the America's Cup Bar in the Hilton feeling a little more relaxed after Gustave's supercharged gins and lime juice. I loosen my tie a bit, unfurl myself, like the wind-filled sails in the pictures on the walls. I whisper into the bar, as neatly as a 28-footer with a good tail wind.

There is a large group of men in the corner. I pull up a bar stool and drop anchor nearby. I order a drink. Waiting, waiting.

At first I can make out only a few of the faces. That surely must be Peter Wolf, his hair heavily receded yet still a brilliant orange, his skin pasty but still freckled. My God. He is not a young old man, or an old young old man, or whatever; he is simply an old, old, old man. What has happened to us in almost thirty years? Is that what I look like?

And is that Simon Little, the Wimbledon contender? The boy who seemed perpetually dressed in whites and Dunlop volley sandshoes? So lithe and athletic at the net? It cannot be. He is fat and as bald as a well-used tennis ball. That cannot be Sam Pauls the swimmer, either. Heavily jowled, beer bellied and big enough to fill a child's backyard paddling pool.

The palms of my hands begin to sweat. The weight of the years king hits me like a freak wave. These are not the people I went to school with. These are different people. Impostors.

Or they are their fathers. Or mothers (Simon Little does have, from this distance at least, what appear to be small breasts).

I finish my drink and quickly order another. I have entered a universe where all the colleagues of my school-days have been taken over by large, dimpled, cellulited aliens. You can still see the boys of my youth inside the aliens: the ghosts of them, the outlines of them, trapped within these strange, bloated external growths. Boys, crying to get out. Pressing their wailing little-boy faces against the translucent membrane of age.

I should slip away now, I think. I should just disappear down the carpeted stairs and never be seen again.

I am just sliding sideways off the stool to make my exit when I am apprehended by a tap on the shoulder. I turn.

The man standing before me is tall and thin and wearing a tweed jacket that has seen better days. He has curly grey-ing hair and sports a Mexican-style moustache that must have been popular when he first grew it in the seventies. A moustache you see on store managers of takeaway pizza outlets in Bum Chafe, Arizona.

His lips part in a smile and that's when I see it. The mali-cious glint that I had seen just before he socked me in the mouth nearly three decades before.

'Sullivan,' he says. 'Remember me?'

How could I forget him? He is the reason I am here, after all.

He had arrived at the school mid-term, out of nowhere, and nobody ever knew anything about him since he kept very much to himself. He possessed a gold tooth. He reminded me of a character out of an Ian Fleming novel.

It was, in fact, the tooth that gave Sullivan his somewhat sinister air. For gold teeth belonged in the mouths of grandfathers or film villains. I had never seen anyone with a gold tooth except in the movies or at the nursing home where my own grandfather resided. Come to think of it, nobody came near my grandfather in the nursing home, with or without a gold tooth. He sat there in silence and alone, his hair always heavily oiled and parted somewhat off-centre. He kept his hands under a crocheted rug, which could very well have concealed a .45.

So it is that when I encounter Sullivan at my school reunion I go into some sort of memory spin. I know it is him and yet it is not him. I put both fists in my pockets. I can recall no advice from my father on the striking of men with gold teeth.

Yet something has happened to Sullivan. Back at school he was like a well-pumped tyre on a racing bicycle. Even his hair looked coiled and sinewy. Now it seems as if someone left the bicycle in the shed for decades, and it has just been brought out into the light as one would retrieve an object from a time machine.

'Sullivan,' I say.

'You,' he says.

It was how Sullivan spoke, way back at school. It was always either 'me' or 'you', 'yes' or 'no'. There were no frills to Sullivan. He was a De Niro gangster before De Niro invented the type.

'Good to see you again,' Sullivan says.

I want to ring Gustave and ask him for an action plan.

I remember what my father said about Frenchmen, and feel I cannot leave Sullivan a note apologising for not being able to fight him on this night.

I decide the direct approach is best.

'The playground,' I say. 'The day you smacked me in the chops for no reason. Do you recall that?' I suddenly feel very foolish.

'I smacked you in the chops?'

'You smacked me in the chops.'

Sullivan pulls up a bar stool. He looks bemused and lost. He grips the bar rail as if to steady himself. Tears fill his eyes.

I have to look away. I sip a very ordinary gin and tonic. Sullivan turns to me.

'I want to apologise for that,' he says.

I don't really hear him. I am too busy thinking of my father's advice and wondering whether, if indeed I did hit Sullivan to even the score after so many years, I would be compelled to kiss him, as is the Australian way. I do not feel Australian, or know what an Australian is, so I feel I am probably excused from that clause. However, Sullivan is taller than me, and if I hit him at all I will still be contravening my father's advice. I had once hit *something* bigger than myself – a restaurant, in my car – but I guess that does not count in my father's code of violence. I must say, in hindsight, that the restaurant came off second best.

'Pardon?'

'I want to apologise for hitting you when I was a kid.'

'Really?'

'I was terribly angry at the time,' whispers Sullivan. 'I was very confused as a teenager.'

'Please, you don't have to explain.'

'It was my . . . my family life, you see. Seven schools in five years. My father, my . . . my . . .'

'Sullivan, it's okay. Please . . .'

'My father was very violent.'

'Was he English?'

'In fact he was,' says Sullivan, looking surprised.

'I thought so.'

I know I have Sullivan, somehow. I have heard a tiny crack, like the breaking of a wishbone, behind our conversation. An almost imperceptible shift of power.

'I . . . I . . .'

I see a tear drop into his cartoon-Mexican moustache. He tries to brush it away.

'Forget it, Sullivan.'

'I felt unloved by my mother. It started when I was 3 years old. I . . .'

There is no stopping Sullivan. He goes on and on.

'Then my sister came along. As you can understand, I was receiving all the attention up to that point . . .'

And on. After forty-five minutes he is only up to the age of 6 in his life story.

'Sullivan, you're forgiven. Forget it.'

'. . . then my father would emerge with this . . . this strap he had made out of . . .'

I can see the rest of the Old Boys having a whale of a time in the corner. The ones as big as whales seem to be having the most fun. Which, if you're having a whale of a time, makes perfect sense. They have even enticed some women into the group, and a large and jolly party is evolving. They are large and, after several drinks, the women are jolly. I want to write this down on one of the America's Cup Bar coasters to tell Gustave later, but I cannot find a clean one, or a pen, and Sullivan simply will not shut up.

'. . . and it was each hit from that strap, each whipping that I remember as clear as yesterday . . .'

'Sullivan,' I say.

'The crack of the leather across my . . .'

'Sullivan.'

'It was so . . . so . . .' he continues, almost sobbing outright.

'Please.'

And that's when I sock him in the jaw.

My swift and inexplicable right to Sullivan's exposed mug proves that my father is wrong. I have hit someone bigger than myself and there are no dire consequences. Also, I have no urge to kiss him. I just want him to stop talking. We have come full circle. It is all over.

As I stand to leave, Sullivan, too, stands and sniffs back his emotions.

'Thank you,' he says.

'My pleasure, Sullivan,' I say, and we shake hands like perfect gentlemen.

I walk out of the bar without saying goodbye – in fact, never having said hello – to anyone.

I return to the Lime Bar and take up my usual stool. Gustave has a gin, lime and tonic prepared in an instant.

I muse to him, 'Isn't it strange, Gustave, how some people like you more the worse you treat them?'

'*Mais oui*,' says Gustave, as if he has known this all his life. 'There are always the people who do the liking, and the people who do the treating. That is the way of the world, *monsieur*.'

'Gustave?'

'*Oui*.'

'What would you do if I ever hit you?'

'Hit me?'

'Yes. How would you react?'

He scratches his chin. 'Perhaps I would slap you across the face with my gloves, *monsieur*.'

'Ah, how very civilised.'

'Then punch you in the – how do you say? – the mug, *monsieur*.'

FIVE

Incident in the Hotel Tangier

FOR three nights running I have sat here in the cocktail lounge of the Hotel Tangier and listened to a singer by the name of Kiki La Monde.

I am growing fond of Kiki. I have already purchased two of her home-recorded cassettes. I will buy another one tonight. If I come tomorrow night, I will buy a fourth.

Yes, I have had a little too much to drink. I make no excuses. I have perhaps become a little over-enthusiastic about the Hotel Tangier's cocktail of the week – the Red Hound – the ingredients of which I have jotted down on the back of a palm-tree-shaped drinks coaster for Gustave, back at the Lime Bar. I think Gustave will find a drink called the Red Hound somewhat amusing.

I have found that the Red Hound actually complements Kiki La Monde. That Kiki and the Hound somehow work together in a way I have yet to understand. She takes away the bitterness of the grapefruit juice. And the Hound brings a certain warmth to her rendition of cocktail-lounge favourites.

I cannot tell you how it stirs me when she closes her eyes and sings that she's daddy's little girl.

During the break in Kiki's set I ponder this theory of drinks going with people, just as some wines belong to individual dishes. Certainly Gustave would not be Gustave without gin and lime juice. When I think of my business partner, Lloyd, I instantly see a tumbler of Scotch on the rocks.

And what of my soon-to-be-ex-wife, Margaret? What of her? She had started out as a crisp and clean local champagne, and ended up as, well, a cold spumante. But I am just being vindictive. It is the bitterness of separation. She is probably in the arms of someone else right now, as supple as a Moët. The Moët that slipped through my fingers.

I have amused myself. I write this down on one of the cardboard fronds of the coaster.

'I'll remember youuuuuuu, alllllwayyyyysssss . . .'

I am astonished that the other patrons of the bar do not recognise Kiki La Monde's versatility. Granted, her orchestral backing music is prerecorded. But her flute and saxophone work, interlaced with her voice, is nothing short of astonishing. I am offended for her by the ill-attention of my fellow drinkers. Kiki is not a canvas backdrop to their idle chatter and boorish flirting. Kiki is not furnishing in the dull drama of their evenings.

'Bravo!' I shout, clapping loudly.

The bar goes silent. You can hear the shift of beer nuts and Indian split peas.

But what the hell. I am here on the Gold Coast in the

Hotel Tangier being pursued by the Red Hound and I am falling in love with a 19-year-old lounge singer called Kiki La Monde, and life for once is good because it is not my life, it is the life of me as a conference-goer on the Gold Coast where I can be anything or anyone I like.

It is what I love about the Gold Coast and why I did not hesitate to register for the South-East Asian Small Traders Conference. It will bring no business. It will produce no valuable contacts. But there are times in life when you have to take leave of yourself for a while. When you're so sick of being *you* that you have to hang up the old 'Back in Five Minutes' sign.

There is no better place to do this than on the Gold Coast. Nothing is real. Nobody is who they seem. This is how I like it.

I have not told my father of the conference. I have never told him anything about my business, not even over golf. My father has dealt in stocks and shares all his life. Not the little fish, but the major stocks that hold up the world economy. He also has a sideline in Australian wheat and wool. My father trades millions of sacks of grain and bales of wool at any given hour. How could I tell him I make money from mass-produced trinkets out of Asia? Against my father's huge dealings, I am a lilliputian business. I deal with little factories and little items that would fit into the pockets of my father's golf bag.

I chose the Hotel Tangier for my conference accommodation because I had a sudden penchant for some North African exotica. I am tickled by the staff in their long and flowing robes, and the fez of the concierge. I have recommended to management that they provide a fez in each room, just as other hotels supply bathrobes and complimentary personal hygiene items. They seem interested in the idea.

I could have booked into a facsimile of Hawaii, or New York, or Munich, or Santorini. All these options were available. But it was, ultimately, the fez that sold the hotel to me.

Lloyd is staying with the other conference-goers, two blocks down in fake Hong Kong. I have attended enough of these things, however, to learn the golden rule of the conference – always avoid the people who actually attend.

I established this maxim early when, as a young man, I was sent to Port Macquarie for a confectionery conference. There was an unsavoury drama, which I won't go into here, involving a Smarties representative from Geelong. And innumerable tiffs and threats of actual violence between sales reps of Violet Crumbles and Turkish delights. This incident is still referred to in confectionery circles. This is what it comes down to, no matter what area of life you move in. Politics. Rank. Teams. One-upmanship. No one, as far as I know, has come up with a more violently imaginative use of a Turkish delight than myself. As far as I know.

I sup on another Red Hound and close my eyes as Kiki La Monde does a reedy but very plausible imitation of Ella Fitzgerald. I applaud warmly. I wonder if there are other singers in smaller bars than that of the Hotel Tangier imitating Kiki La Monde.

'Encore!'

Someone tosses a pretzel in my direction.

I am not against the notion of conferences. They have given me much over the years. My friend and occasional golfing partner Oliver says he goes to at least one conference annually for a personal and private nervous breakdown, which, in the end, he can write off on tax.

In fact, Oliver's method is quite unique and has been passed on, with success, to other close friends. He shuts himself in his room, draws the blinds and plays, over and over, the video of the film *Titanic*. He starts the video well past the 'I'm king of the world' quip. He commences viewing when the ship first strikes the iceberg, then, in the dark, listens to the ensuing disaster at close to full volume. He says this brings on his breakdown and excises his stress in an economical fashion. 'If you've been to the bottom,' he says rather obviously, 'there's only one way to go.' I have always felt Oliver is a trifle over-dramatic. And his behaviour in a golf-course bunker has to be seen to be believed.

I have learned much, also, about human behaviour at conferences. I know that people can fall in love very quickly when removed from the routine of their own normal environment. I have seen astounding couplings that would never have been considered beyond the borders of the conference. I have seen people tumble into frenetic affairs by virtue of being paired with a surname alphabetically close to their own. Over time I have observed this method of mating – the As and Bs stick together, the Cs and Ds. It's as good a way of getting together as any. (I don't want to think of the problems involved amongst the WXYZs.)

Kiki La Monde is moving around the bar with her satchel of cassettes. I admire her confidence. I admire her self-belief. I admire her young cleavage.

'Good evening,' she says sweetly, approaching my table.

'Well, good evening.'

'Would you care to buy —'

But I am ahead of her. I have the wallet open.

'Twenty-five dollars?'

'Yes,' she says, surprised.

'I love your work,' I say, smiling, and wonder how many millions of men around the world have said 'I love your work' to a woman in the past few hours.

'Why, thank you,' she says, passing me the cassette of *Kiki La Monde's Warm Evenings*.

I tuck the cassette in the pocket of my sports jacket. I am feeling considerably warm inside. No matter that Kiki has brought her wares to my banquette three nights in a row and still does not recognise me from the nights before. This is a place where everything starts afresh at dawn.

'Would you like a cocktail?' I ask, but she has already gone.

I order a final Red Hound from the waiter and notice Kiki across the room in conversation with the barman. They are both looking at me discreetly. I smile and give a small wave. Kiki waves back. I look away coolly and hum a riff from 'Always'.

I down my drink and leave the bar. Kiki has finished for the evening. The barman is polishing his glasses. I knock into a plastic palm tree on the way out but don't think anyone notices. I stand unsteadily at the lift and see my distorted face in the brass plate behind the lift buttons.

I sit for a moment in the dark, on the balcony of my room overlooking the beach, and am refreshed by the sea breeze.

I am about to break the second rule of conference-going: never go swimming in the hotel pool whilst drunk.

I don't foresee any drama. I am not, after all, at the official conference hotel, with its own official conference pool and spa where official conference-goers could be, at this very moment, fondling foreign genitals beneath a screen of spa-jet bubbles. I am in the Hotel Tangier, heading down in the lift in my fluffy white Hotel Tangier bathrobe to a pool shimmering just beyond imitation rustic red-and-white-brick Moroccan colonnades. I tap my bare foot on the lift carpet. I emit a grapefruity belch.

I am alone in the pool. I float on my back and think of Kiki La Monde and see her emerging naked from the dark wooden sauna in a fine haze of steam and the scent of pine needles.

I gently knock my head against the edge of the pool, right myself, and, incredibly, she is there, at the far end, in her tight black Kiki La Monde cocktail dress.

'Kiki,' I say, and her name echoes off the brick arches: 'Kiki, iki, iki, ki, ki, i.'

'May I join you?'

She does not wait for my answer. She simply slips off her dress and enters the pool in nothing but a pale pink G-string. She swims slowly towards me, loops her hands around my neck, and kisses me gently.

48

'Kiki,' I say. I do not comprehend the situation. I have a vague and somewhat unformed notion that it has to do with the number of copies of *Warm Evenings* I have purchased.

She leads me into the spa, where I sit uncomfortably close to a jet. I am rigid, not with fear, but with surprise at the infinite turns that life takes.

'I love your work,' I say woodenly. Kiki La Monde plays with my knobbly knees under the water.

'So how long have you been with Sony?'

I think she asks, How long is your pony? But I cannot be sure. The hairs on my legs and thighs are erect and tingling in the seething water.

'Pardon?'

'Sony. How long have you been with them?'

Sony. Sony. This word registers with me somewhere. I try to reach through the fog of the Red Hounds and retrieve it. It takes several long minutes but it finally comes to me. I remember the 'Welcome to the Hotel Tangier' sandwich board in the foyer. Sony. Sony. It is a gross case of mistaken identity. I have accidentally been consumed by another conference.

'About five years,' I say.

And Kiki La Monde slides both hands into the legs of my complimentary Hong Kong Handover '97 swimming trunks.

SIX

The Death of Canasta

I AM having what Gustave calls 'a trot of the bad'.

It is one of many phrases, lost to time, that Gustave has filed beneath his shamelessly old-fashioned twenties Brylcreemed-and-swept-back hairstyle. (I have dubbed it his anti-antimacassar.)

He will say things are 'not flash', or that something was like 'the tickets pakapoo'.

Ordinarily I relish Gustave's wisdom and his consolation. They echo to me from somewhere long ago, across the linoleum of my Great-aunt Dot's kitchen or the leather-rich cabin of my grandfather's Buick.

But when I return from my conference on the Gold Coast, following the incident in the Hotel Tangier, Gustave's intuitive, sympathetic glance acts not as a balm but as a reminder that I have lost my youth.

I cannot blame Gustave. He knows nothing of my case of mistaken identity in the swimming pool of the Hotel Tangier, and the amorous approaches of the hotel cabaret singer,

Ms Kiki La Monde. He may never know unless, as seems likely, I slip through the crack in his fine gin and limes, and confess all.

He may be suspicious of my hasty return from the conference. I have gone straight from the airport to the Lime Bar, complete with tagged luggage. Nevertheless, he shows the good manners not to ask anything.

Normally, I would say something. Gustave, like all good barmen, is a receptacle of oral autobiography. Behind that shiny forehead, there is a giant tablet on which all the details of my life are transcribed.

'Boswell, have you packed for Scotland?' I will often exclaim to him late in the evening, and he will laugh too loudly, in the way people do when they have misheard or misunderstood a joke, or wish to acknowledge a gag without finding it remotely funny.

Yet now, having returned from the Hotel Tangier, I remain purse-lipped. There, in my room overlooking the Surfers Paradise beach, I had encountered my own reality. Most people toil all their lives hoping to meet themselves. Spend thousands of dollars on therapy. Keep an entire global industry alive. But it is the journey they want in their lives, not the end result. My psychiatrist has often told me, honest chap that he is, that when we get close to my own reality, I should change therapists.

I tell my therapist I have the exact same theory about men and women. That we lose interest in each other not necessarily because of a sexual waning, or a change in direction. It's just that we've run out of story. The partner knows everything. All recollections. All warm and meaning-ful remembrances. All embarrassments. We leave people, I say, to find a fresh set of ears and to start all over again.

We had played in the hotel pool like children, Kiki La Monde and I. She in her G-string, and I in my baggy Hong Kong Handover '97 swimming trunks, my genitals covered by the Chinese flag, my buttocks by the Union Jack.

She had asked me about my taste in music and had found it enormously funny that I favoured a forgotten Tasmanian band called MEO245. She considered this rather 'hip'. It proved, on reflection, how creaky I had become – the pecu-liar alchemy of things mundane in their time ultimately appearing 'hip'.

It was, I think, the admission about MEO245 that opened the door of Kiki La Monde's trust and intimacy, since it was she who suggested we retire to my room. As we travelled together in the elevator, the pool water sprinkling the carpet, I had the enormously uplifting revelation that I was still attractive to young women, that I still 'had it', as middle-aged men often say. (I chose, in my drunkenness, to ignore the deception on which all this was based – that Kiki La Monde had mistaken me for a senior recording company executive.)

I fumbled with the door key, then finally waved her inside my room. A strange, disquieting giggle issued from my person. She did not seem to notice.

It was, of course, an instant disaster. I had been too caught up in the notion of Kiki La Monde's firm young but-tocks, and other regions, even to anticipate the windfall deception, let alone properly architect the lie. For there, laid out on my bed, were the several souvenirs and samples I had taken from the South-East Asian Small Traders Conference – a little mounted Hong Kong junk, a series of Sydney Opera House salt and pepper shakers, and three glow-in-the-dark Hula-hoops from Korea.

I had, as Gustave would have said, behaved like 'a goose's wigwam for a bridle'.

It had taken Kiki La Monde just seconds to realise her error. I quickly turned on the stereo and played *Warm Evenings* to keep her in the room. But even before her flute solo in 'Georgia' had reached its crescendo, she was gone.

'Kiki!' I shouted down the corridor.

'You sleazy old bastard,' she called back, over her shoulder.

I sat up for hours and watched the sunrise. I had become everything I thought I would never be. I was an incumbent divorcee, and 'sleazy'.

I tried to look at the situation from the reverse angle. Which sorts of women would be attracted to a middle-aged man? If they were young, would they want something in exchange, as had Kiki La Monde? Or would they be of that select and rather minuscule group that needed a replacement father? Would they desire that maturity? (Gustave's words echoed in my head: 'Ah, *monsieur*, when do we ever throw off the *enfants*?') At the other end of the scale, would they be older women who desired companionship, a figure across the breakfast table, a warm lump in bed, without the complications of a relationship? Would I end up just filling a space? A cardboard cut-out, hoisted under the arm and propped up in a room, bent onto a dining chair, anchored to the front lawn with a watering hose clipped to my flat hand?

The countless probabilities depressed me. I returned to Sydney with haste, leaving my Kiki La Monde cassettes for the housemaid.

'You are having a bad trot?' Gustave finally asks me.

'Life is a pakapoo ticket.'

'Every racehorse must turn the corner.'

I begin to wonder what has happened to Gustave in my absence. I am puzzled by his analogies of the track, and suspect the jockeys' collective has discovered the Lime Bar while I have been away. I do not need, at this moment, to have my favourite bar infiltrated by local jockeys, riding the high pale-timber stools into the early hours.

'Here,' Gustave says, 'change your luck.' And with that, he tosses me half a dozen betting chips. 'The casino, the Star City, it is open now. Go.'

I study the chips.

'Go, go,' Gustave says, shooing me from the bar. 'Change your trot.'

I don't know why I obey Gustave. Perhaps it is the perishing of my self-esteem. It has wheezed out of me since the incident in the Hotel Tangier, as high-pitched as a leak in a volleyball bladder.

Leaving my suitcase in Gustave's care, I take a cab directly to Darling Harbour, and within ten minutes I am playing blackjack with several Cantonese chefs who have just finished their shift in Chinatown.

I suddenly feel warm and wanted inside, snug at the

horseshoe table. I am enveloped in soft light and the aroma of seared scallops and sizzling beef rising from the Cantonese chefs.

My lucky streak lasts for over two hours, during which I befriend the chefs and even, at the end, receive from them several recipes for barbecued pork and a secret Peking duck sauce. My spirits have lifted immeasurably.

Then, in an aisle of poker machines, I encounter her.

How could I have known that, within the space of a single day, I would farewell a woman of my past youth, namely Kiki La Monde, and encounter a woman of my future, namely Gladys – grandmother, poker-machine addict, former New South Wales canasta champion, and cider drunk?

As I sit playing a poker machine that features jungle animals, her meek pleading comes to me through the chatter of toucans.

'Excuse me, young man,' she says, 'could you help me?'

I turn to see a sort of miniature version of Drysdale's Drover's Wife, all hat and handbag. She looks like a strange antique lampshade in the razzle-dazzle of Star City.

'I've had a bit of a bad trot,' she says. 'Could you buy me a glass of cider?'

And I do. I buy her several ciders. I hear the story of Gladys, and how the death of canasta has ruined her life and robbed her of her self-worth. How canasta had given her life meaning. How its wane in popularity has deprived her of friendships and continuity.

'They were lovely times,' she says. 'Oh, the kings and queens. The jacks and aces. And the dear little jokers. My, to have a handful of jokers, my boy. It set the heart racing, it did.'

She recounts how, in the end, she would play for hours by herself – indeed, against herself – and in these times at the formica-topped kitchen table she imagined her invisible opponent as a young Gladys, a vibrant woman in her twenties all pancaked and rouged, with an ear to the street and the car horn that would signal the arrival of her gentleman friend on a Saturday evening.

'I used to tango,' she says around the ciggie hanging out of the corner of her mouth, her lined and powdered face glowing like ivory in the light from the poker machine. 'But that disappeared, too.'

I sit with Gladys in the Star City Casino until dawn, and feed her poker-machine addiction, and watch her graduate from a single machine to playing two at once, her hat swivelling from side to side, her large buttocks spilling over the edges of the stool.

She is in both the Wild West and Medieval Europe. A coyote howls from the machine to her right. A lute plunks to her left.

When I run out of money Gladys moves on. She finds someone else in the next aisle to buy her a cider. I can hear, in the pauses between the machines' cries and honks, her eulogy on the death of canasta.

I recall how, as a child, I watched my parents playing the game with friends, and felt confused by the bitterness that often rose from the table as slowly and tangibly as the smoke from my mother's perpetual menthol cigarettes. There was,

I was later told, a marriage disintegration that stemmed not from infidelity or lack of care and attention, but a simple yet crucial dispensing of a card on the discard deck during one of my parents' epic tournaments.

'She's all in the turn of the card, boy,' my father once told me, referring presumably to life. I viewed canasta with great suspicion.

Later, when the crowds of the tennis set opted for a canasta night, I initially refused to play. I was still very young, and I had seen the game's ability to extract the personalities of its players, to strip bare the essence of a person. Bullish or patient? Quietly cunning or bombastically aggressive? Hare or tortoise?

I was partnered with Margaret that night. I had not a notion then of any form of coupling. Nevertheless, there we were for the evening, a canasta team against the world. I should have paid more attention. She dealt and received cards with a sort of grace that transcended the table. She found my errors amusing, the rising heat from other partner-ships something to be gently doused, the outcome irrelevant. She failed to have a single competitive bone in her body and saw the game for exactly what it was – just a game.

Her gentle amusement at the entire scenario quickly transferred to me. We chortled and nudged each other's ribs with our elbows through the unending match. She feigned seriousness at times, which made us even more hysterical. At one point she slipped out of the room and returned wearing a tennis visor, to deal the deck with an exaggerated profession-alism that even had the others laughing.

Of course, having rejected the game's more dangerously inherent motives, having shucked the combativeness of it all, we won.

'So who's for coffee?' she said as soon as the points were declared, pecking me on the cheek as she left for the kitchen. It was all there in front of me at that table. Margaret did not need a game to draw out her nature. She never hid it in the first place.

I see Gladys through the gap in the poker machines. And I think, this is it. I no longer have a chance for romance. I am like canasta: nobody wants to play me any more.

SEVEN

The Strange Ways of Mountain Men

I AM convinced my psychiatrist needs a psychiatrist.

As I sit here around a camp fire high in the Australian Alps with seven American tourists, our trail guide and a bandy camp cook, I only just realise, after all the months of therapy, how odd it is that my psychiatrist also takes to a couch during his interrogations.

I cannot believe it has never struck me as peculiar until now. The way both couches in his wood-panelled suite are positioned parallel, like two tourist buses in a car park. The way he always reclines diametrically opposed to me, his feet in line with my head, my feet with his head.

We casually gaze across at each other, like two old English gents who have found themselves in an Algerian steam house. He speaks as if he is my friend. He must be. He is always saying, 'I am your friend here.' As he checks his watch.

Perhaps this is his 'method'. To mirror me, and make me feel less anxious. Perhaps he is saying to me: There is nothing wrong with you. We are the same, you and I.

But we are not the same. Our wallets are not the same when I leave his office. And he always, *always*, wears white socks, as if a few sets of tennis are imminent.

That, at least, is one thing I have learned dozens of sessions and hundreds of dollars later: white socks do not look good with suit pants.

I hear cars honking in the distance and I am brought back, back to the camp fire, and realise they are not car horns at all, but cattle lost somewhere in the dark scrub, studded through the ghostly snow gums way up here, in the Australian Alps.

'Another beer?'

It is Bunger, the trail guide.

'Sorry?'

'Beer. You want another one?'

I look towards him and can barely see his face beneath the large, nibbled brim of his rabbit-skin hat. It reminds me of the annexe of the family caravan of my friend Douglas during my boyhood vacations by the sea. I would visit Douglas every day in the caravan park – 'Now don't have lunch there,' my mother would say. 'We must be mindful of germs.' – and return at dusk to our suite in a hotel on the hill. From the balcony I would look down at the twinkling kerosene lanterns scattered through the caravan park, golden stars that shivered beyond ropes and sheets of canvas. I longed for the intimacy of the vans and the tents.

'Thank you.'

It all started, this ridiculous horse-riding epic, this journey into the Snowy Mountains, when I mentioned to my therapist the death of canasta, and Gladys in the Star City Casino, and the realisation that I had, as a man, entered the void of the unlovable, the unwanted, and that in the great long corridor of life I had reached the quiet end of the wing.

'Nonsense,' he said. 'I assume you have written this twaddle on one of your drinks coasters.'

He always says 'Nonsense.' And 'Bah.' I prefer 'Nonsense' to 'Bah.' 'Bah' always makes me feel like a child. For some reason Winston Churchill instantly comes to mind when he says 'Bah', and I have many nightmares where Winston Churchill is actually my father, and each Churchill nightmare is the same. I am always in bed, and there is a rap on the door, and he comes in to wish me goodnight, and the long, rectangular shadow of his greatcoat falls over me, and the glowing tip of his cigar grows and grows as he gets closer, until it is so close and huge and red that I feel I have fallen into hell.

I never mention my Churchill nightmare to my psychiatrist. Instead, I secretly hope he has a Famous Person Nightmare of his own – perhaps one in which the giant white socks of Rod Laver or Martina Navratilova bear down on his minuscule self.

'You are suffering a delusion most common to men facing divorce,' he concluded. 'In fact, I am glad you're now going in this direction, and not the other.'

'What is the other?'

'The Compensatory Machismo Route.'

'Machismo Route?'

'The I'll-screw-as-many-women-as-I-can-to-prove-my-worth axiom.'

'That doesn't sound so bad to me.'

'Let me tell you, it's bad.'

'You're telling me the I-have-nothing-to-come-home-to-but-the-cat-and-a-cold-can-of-lemon-peppered-tuna is the better route of the two routes?'

'It is the better route.'

'I'm tired of all the route talk.'

'Bah.' He wriggled his toes within his white socks. 'Nevertheless, I think it is essential you reacquaint yourself with your maleness.'

'Reacquaint?'

'In light of the incident at the Hotel Tangier, where you became, shall we say, entangled in the perils of the-older-almost-divorced-man-seeks-the-attentions-of-the-hopelessly-younger-woman syndrome —'

'Not route?'

'Please don't interrupt. Then you followed this up with the confrontation in the casino, where you clearly suffered the oh-no-my-future-is-nothing-but-a-barren-wasteland-of-older-women projection. My advice to you is to go away, perhaps to the mountains, and get in touch with your primal masculinity.'

'I go to the Gold Coast for that, for Christ's sake.'

'Nonsense. I am ordering you to return to the earth. To the real earth. To get dirty. To swing yourself onto a horse. To swig from the water bottle attached to your hip. To eat smoky toast for breakfast . . .'

His toe-wiggling slowed at this point. He drifted into a light slumber and I left quietly.

And as is always my way with his most ridiculous suggestions, his most ludicrous hypotheses, I took his advice, and booked myself on a five-day trail ride into the Australian Alps.

Before I had even embarked on this odyssey, I was rewarded with benefits.

One lunch hour, just days before I was due to leave, I happened upon an army disposal store I had never previously noticed (my psychiatrist would see something significant here, no doubt) and decided, in an instant, to apparel myself for the trail.

It was, quite frankly, a revelation. The infinite accoutrements for the outdoor man. The myriad outfits and objects to clip onto your belt, and belts onto which things could be clipped, and secret pockets and compartments and chambers for the tools of survival. I was overcome by the perfume of canvas, and wondered if this response had always been a part of man's genetic make-up, reawoken in times such as this, in moments of threat and crisis.

I stood in the camouflage-waterproof-vest section and felt tears welling in my eyes. I thought of Douglas, my lost friend, and heard bugs pop against hot lantern glass and the creak of bunks echo about me.

More than two hours later I came out of the store laden with knives and boots and pannikins and quart water bottles and an alpine pack and even a small plastic box of fishing flies for which I had no rod or line. The whole business of being enclosed in this cave of maleness had lifted my spirits immeasurably.

I flew to Albury–Wodonga, feeling fully equipped and infinitely younger than my years, and hired a four-wheel drive. The next day I drove to the property where the trail began. I walked towards the horse yard and my travelling companions for the next five days with a confidence that had been missing in my life for too long.

I shook hands firmly with Bunger and Curly, the camp cook, and before I knew it was astride my horse, my ark for this crucial journey – a filly called Dentures – and looking into the blue-green mountains with a deeply disguised childlike anticipation.

I had forgotten, up to this point, that I had not ridden a horse since I was eleven. A pony, in fact, at a friend's birthday party. As a child I mixed in the sort of circles that always featured ponies at birthday parties. I did not, at the time, view it as an extravagance, nor did I question the reason for having a pony at a birthday party. Before the video games, drugs and violence that are now the standard indulgence for children aged 11, I guess a pony was the maximum excitement. How we have changed so dramatically in our appreciation of things. Surely the only enduring pleasure not superseded is sex. I shall have to ask Gustave. He would know about sex. At present he would know a lot more than me. Perhaps not so much about ponies. (But you never know with Gustave, let alone the French.)

Having thought these profound thoughts within a minute of being seated on Dentures, I began to view my psychiatrist's advice more leniently. Perhaps he knew what he was talking about for once. I gripped the reins.

'Rightio then,' said Bunger, and suddenly we were off, the horses filing behind each other, carrying me and the Americans, while Curly shot ahead in a four-wheel drive and trailer.

There was little talk in the first hour as we loped in a single line through paddocks to the foot of the mountains. I observed the Americans for any indication of their riding prowess or, more accurately, their lack of it. I wanted at least one of them to be as inept as myself.

Yet I found no signs of the novice amongst the visitors. They shifted as naturally in the saddle as if they had been born to it. They wore grubby cowboy hats and riding helmets that had obviously already suffered the rigours of past trails. They were all decked out in riding pants, with either leather calf-protectors or high boots.

I, on the other hand, had simply worn jeans and mountain-hiking boots. In my excitement at the army disposal store, I had forgotten to ask about equestrian fineries. Before we had even reached the base of the ranges the insides of my lower legs were painfully chafed. Each step taken by Dentures made them feel like they were being fed into a sausage mincer. Or what I assumed a sausage mincer felt like, since I was an afficionado of mobster movies, especially those that featured sausage mincers.

It was only four hours to Curly's camp site.

By a small creek at the bottom of the mountain we were to climb that afternoon, we spelled the horses, then let them drink. I was already in agony.

'You okay back there?' Bunger hollered. I waved him the all clear as Dentures noisily sucked in water like a teenager finishing off the dregs of a milkshake through a straw.

'Good-o then,' said Bunger, and we started our ascent.

It is the way of the mountains and the bush, I discovered later, that horses are named either willy-nilly – Sugar, Rosy, Clancy – or because they reveal some significant characteristic early in their short lives. Within hours I realised why my filly had been dubbed Dentures.

As we started the climb, the muscles rippling beneath the shiny coats of these powerful mountain horses, Dentures began snapping at the posterior of the horse in front.

'Don't do that,' I instructed Dentures. She simply snorted, and then proceeded to try to push her entire head into the horse's derrière.

This was my first test of reacquainting myself with my manhood, and I attempted to show Dentures who was boss. 'Good Dentures,' I whispered in a sort of mantra. 'Atta girl, Dentures.'

Yet no matter how often I tugged the reins straight back or steered her head away from the rump of the horse in front, she gnashed and stamped and chewed on her bit until I relented.

By mid-afternoon we finally reached Curly's camp, and I swivelled off Dentures and rocked, on wishbone legs, towards the camp fire and the relief of a canvas stool.

Now, several hours later, when I have still not moved, Bunger comes over and sits on the log beside me and passes me a can of beer.

'How's your legs?' he asks, looking into the fire.

'Pretty average.'

'Shoulda worn stockings. Didn't they tell ya to bring stockings?'

I do not remember any stockings department in the army disposal store.

'No, they didn't.'

'Gotta wear stockings if you haven't ridden for a while.'

Finally I relax, and am enjoying the bonhomie of the mountains when Bunger opens another can.

'Can't sleep in a normal bed no more,' he says. 'Only sleep outdoors now. The wife and me are bluein' at the moment anyhow . . .'

'I'm sorry.'

'Like it up here, round the camp. Like to be with me mates. You know what I'm sayin'?'

Night falls, and the fire flickers in his eyes. And all I can think of is Bunger and Curly wearing sheer black stockings underneath their dungarees.

I am close to touching my manhood. And, I suspect, my manhood is close to being touched.

EIGHT

Bluey's Blues

ON my third night by the camp fire I begin to develop strange and improper thoughts that have no place in the Australian Alps.

I could blame Rudy, head janitor of the Miami Dolphins' football stadium, and the vast quantities of sour mash we share.

I had not expected to make friends on my five-day horse trek into the fabled Snowy Mountains. In the words of my psychiatrist, my purpose is to 'earth' myself, like some lunatic electrical wire gone mad, and forget about my failed search for love.

Yet it is difficult not to like an American who always introduces himself in full as 'Rudy, head janitor of the Miami Dolphins' football stadium'.

There is also something quaint about his enormous range of Miami Dolphins apparel, clean sets of which he displays each morning and evening by the camp fire.

Nothing he wears is without the dolphin insignia – caps,

sunglasses, shirts, trousers, shorts, shoes, drinking canteen, a knife in a leather holster – and as we hit the horseback trail on the first day it had been almost spiritual the way Rudy's dolphin logos eased effortlessly through the harsh Australian scrub, seemingly leaping and frolicking in an ocean of gum leaves.

He fitted snugly into my view of Americans. It is a subject Gustave and I have often debated. To me, Americans have a deliciously attractive just-hatched-out-of-the-egg quality, a naïveté that emerges with each new experience. They will fondle, say, a bill of foreign currency as if it were the first-ever bill of currency they had held in their hands. Their mouths form a largish 'O', their eyebrows lift, and they proceed to discuss its merits at length. Everything, to Americans, has merit. Everything, to Americans, can be sourced to the goodness of God. I am positive Adam and Eve were Americans.

'Pfffttt!' exclaims Gustave, in his typical, spitological French manner.

'Then why do they have such large and good teeth?'

'*Pardon*?'

'Americans. It's all those apples. You see? Adam and Eve.'

'You are a very silly man sometimes.'

Gustave insists they are a nation of sexless, cultureless morons intent on destroying the world. It is difficult to debate Gustave's proposition. When someone ends a point with an emphatic French pfffttt, there is no adequate response in the English language.

Trek leader Bunger and his sidekick, Curly, had immediately

looked upon Rudy with something beyond distaste. They designated to him the toughest mountain horse in the valley – Snort – as a means, one can only presume, of hosing down his American effervescence.

Yet Rudy handled Snort with ease, confiding in me later that he had once been head janitor of the Denver Broncos' football stadium, and that part of his duties had been to ride the club mascot – a horse, of course – around the field after each touchdown. The Broncos won a place in the play-offs in the year of Rudy's tenure, so he packed in some serious riding hours.

The excellent quality of his sour mash may have something to do with our friendship as well.

Whilst the rest of the group, including Bunger and Curly, crack cans of beer in the firelight on this our third night, Rudy and I savour a most excellent bourbon and dry, complemented by the slightly bent but otherwise superlative Cubans I had tucked into the top pocket of my special camouflage-green safari vest before leaving for my outdoors adventure.

'Thems gooooood,' says Rudy, in a voice made velvety by our after-dinner treats.

'Thems is,' I say.

And as waves of our thick and luxuriant cigar smoke roll through the firelight, I detect a distinct and growing shift of attitude in Bunger and Curly.

Where they had been Captains of the Bush on the first two nights, they are now sullen and unexpectedly pernickety. We are becoming familiar with our surroundings. Members of the group have even discovered a nearby stream, and have gambolled naked in its fern-fringed pools. Bunger and Curly are no longer the experts on all things Bush.

I also sense that the presence of Rudy's and my glass mash tumblers and the Cubans have caused a rift in our party. That we have introduced unwelcome objects into the orbit of the camp fire. The glint of cut glass and the exotic aroma of the cigar leaf have created a division between us, as clean as a steel fence post hammered into rock.

'That horse dung you got wrapped in those things?' Bunger asks of the cigars. He never takes his eyes from the fire.

'From the best thoroughbred,' I say.

'Damn!' Rudy says, slapping his thigh. I always like people who laugh at my jokes.

'Smells like brumby crap to me. How about you, Curly?'

'Yeah. Brumby crap.'

'Finest brumby crap in all of Havana,' I say. 'Many brumbies around here, Bunger?'

'Few.'

'Let's go find some tomorrow. I'd like to light up a couple, see how they compare.'

Rudy's entire body shakes and he spills some of his mash onto the grass. The other American tourists remain silent.

It is a terrible quality in me that I have not seen or heard since I was a university student. It is something released only by considerable amounts of bourbon. It is the sarcastic beast, its flanks covered in thick, bristling hairs, its eyes as cold as ice chunks from an ancient glacier, its evil fathomless.

I can see Bunger's wire-thin lips turn up in a half-smile,

but he is not amused. He has that excruciating look of quick-tempered men who, due to circumstances, have to contain themselves, and his whole being thrums with the effort of it. Ridges of muscle appear along his forearms.

At this moment I loathe everything about the Australian bush and the fly-filled air of superiority these mountain men carry with them. To them the bush *is* Australia, and anything that is not the bush, or born in or of it, is a fraud.

Just as I am about to unleash another of my ripostes, a figure enters the circle of firelight.

'Here's Bluey,' says Bunger, addressing the tourist party. 'He's the mad bugger I told you about. He's gonna sing us some songs.'

'Bunger, Curly,' says Bluey. 'Evenin' everyone.'

Bluey, of course, wears a blue trucker's singlet. He is accompanied, of course, by a blue cattle dog. He has, as far as I can tell, carrot-red hair. Of course. A packet of Champion tobacco is tucked into the plaited band around his filthy hat. Bluish booze veins net his nose.

'How come they call you Bluey?' I ask. There is no reply.

He sits on a log and tunes his guitar – it looks like an oversized ukelele – and there is a titter of excitement from all the Americans except Rudy. I can see the dolphin on Rudy's cap jiggling silently.

'Thought I'd play ya some real Aussie bush songs,' says Bluey.

Bunger looks towards me. He seems more confident now that Bluey has arrived, and crushes an empty beer can beneath his boot as if to emphasise this.

'None of that Yank stuff up here, isn't that right, Bluey?'

The Americans laugh at this sarcasm at their expense, as Americans do on foreign soil. It seems a relaxed luxury, afforded to a race that knows it is the most powerful on earth. This is another of Gustave's points – that the world exists to amuse Americans. 'We are the playpen, *monsieur*,' he often says, 'around which they throw their twinkie things and cups of Coca-Cola. Pfffttt!'

But I can tell from Bunger's smirk that he no longer considers me an Australian either. That I have at some point become very un-Australian in my manner, and thus a traitor. Or worse. That I have drifted beyond nationality, unable to secure a berth anywhere, like the constantly circling satellites in the skies above us. I puff more urgently on the Cuban.

'This is a little song I wrote . . .' Bluey says, strumming, and he proceeds to sing in the most extraordinary Irish twang. It is such a rich and instant transition that it strikes me as some sort of ventriloquist's trick. It is like having a dog scamper up to you and meow. It is unnerving.

'Oh me lovely Mary-Annnne, I remember you standin' on the pier, your eyes black pools of teaarrrrsss . . .'

I wince through my cigar smoke. My eyes water. I know exactly what the lovely Mary-Anne was feeling.

The Americans applaud politely when Bluey finishes. He rolls a Champion, and I think about why he has suddenly gone from being the butcher in Jindabyne that he is to some moon-eyed Limerick-bog-farmer-turned-bushwhacker, and I realise up here in the mountains with the Americans this is our only historical identity, this rag-bag of billy cans and Irish-born bushrangers and gum trees, this thin pastiche of dusty fleeces, and utes, and dogs in neckerchiefs. It's as if this is all we have – slab huts, and the creaking bush, and the music of beer belches.

'This is another one of me own numbers,' Bluey says. ''S about an Aussie bushranger called Captain Moonlight.'

Rudy nearly fires a mouthful of sour mash into the fire. Droplets crackle and hiss on the burning logs.

'Wish I was born a hundred years agooooo . . .' sings Bluey.

'Fairntairstic,' one of the American tourists announces, applauding the rebel Bluey, who rolls another Champion.

'S'pose the night wouldn't be complete without a rendition of "The Man from Snowy River" . . .'

'Yerrr,' the tourists say in unison.

It dawns on me then that this is what they have come for. This is why these people have flown halfway round the world to suffer unbearable heat and be attacked by horse flies and eat fatty steaks cooked over a smoking fire. They have come to be part of some movie they saw years before. Some concocted narrative based not even on a real person – in Snowy River country that is not even Snowy River country in the movie, but some hillocks to the south, kilometres away from the once-legendary river.

I emit an accidental groan.

'That okay with you, pal?' Bluey asks.

'Sure,' I say.

Rudy pulls down the peak of his cap.

'There was movement at the station, for the word had passed around . . .'

I blame my psychiatrist. Staring up at the stars, I decide that for a month after I return I will only answer his questions with lines from Banjo Paterson poems. Every loping, lumbering and cantering line I can remember and feel is appropriate.

As Bluey drones on, I evolve a theory that it is Banjo who has caused all this. It is Banjo who has made a farce of the bush. It is Banjo who, a hundred years later, still fills the egos and self-images of these mountain men as enthusiastically as a camper pumping air into a mattress. It is Banjo who still has people writing reams of rhyming couplets at kitchen tables in rural houses right across Australia.

'And the stockmen tell the story of his ride . . . There ya go.'

Curly snores quietly against his swag. Bunger crushes another can. I relight my Cuban.

'Fairntairstic,' the Americans say.

I wonder about all these men being men together high up in the ranges, splashing water at each other in streams of melted snow, bedding down side by side near the dying coals of a fire, winking and touching the brims of their hats and saying everything by saying nothing. It is like some flyblown open-air Masonic Lodge.

Ignoring Bluey's final original recitation of cutting the tails from lambs (what he rhymes with 'merino' I don't care to know), I lose myself in the stars, and under the heavy influence of Rudy's corn mash succumb to a deep melancholy.

I stare into the constellations and believe, for a moment, that the entire Milky Way is dominated by a woman's stiletto shoe. I rub my eyes and check again. It is still there.

'. . . off with yer tail, me lovely, its fleece so warm and cuddly . . .'

I remember the long, sleek, stockinged foot of Jane, a neighbour when Margaret and I had been married a few years, and the evening of the steamboat we all shared. It is the biggest problem with the bush. Too many ghosts. Everyone's past is out here, peeling off tree trunks, growing on stream rocks, flitting across the sky.

The stiletto of stars glitters, and I am back at that dining table with Jane's foot sliding up and down my ankle unbeknown to anyone but ourselves. I remember how that unexpected motion had set off such an unbelievable chain of events.

And I think, suddenly very alone, how something as delicate as the brush of thistledown on a breeze, a touch so brief, can bring down the human heart, as dynamite can bring down a mountain.

Romeo y Julieta

MY father smokes Romeo y Julieta cigars.

I am unsure when he actually graduated to the Romeo y Julieta. It must have been late in a life I have always measured by cigars.

He started with Wee Willems when I was a child. They were so familiar to me I wanted to be called Wee Willem. I thought this would endear me to my father. That it would admit me into his veil of blue smoke.

I was a teenager when he shifted to Café Crèmes. I liked the short plastic butts of the Crèmes. The feel of the smooth plastic between your lips. He offered one to me from the tin when I graduated from school. I thought this would be the moment I moved closer to my father. It wasn't. The tin was never opened to me again.

Eventually the Romeo y Julietas arrived. They produced even more impenetrable smoke than the Willems and the Crèmes. I hovered on its fringe and waited for it to envelop me. It didn't.

In the Romeo range he preferred the Cedros de Luxe No. 2, or the Cazadores, imported from his favourite cigar dealer – Desmond Sautter of Mayfair, London. He had started off on the San Cristobal de la Habana, but complained that the leaf was rolled too loosely, which he blamed on the state of the Cuban economy, and ultimately the US government's attitude to all things Cuban. Through Mr Sautter, he purchased numerous cigar accoutrements, including a Davidoff Twin-Blade Guillotine.

Years later I learned why some cigars have such romantic names. They originated on the factory floor. To relieve the workers' boredom with rolling thousands of cigars, the supervisors read them passages from Shakespeare or *The Count of Monte Cristo*. I liked the symmetry of this. I imagined all those words encased in tobacco leaf.

It is the cigar that has ultimately given me the key to my father. This small cylinder of pleasure – able to be slipped into the top pocket, kept alive by your own breath, producing every time its unique blue and swirling screen to the world – this has been my father's undoing.

Less than six months ago my father, respected businessman, golf club committee member, confidante of the Lord Mayor and possessor of his own private box at the football stadium, was exposed as a philanderer. He was in his midseventies. Cara, the object of his attentions, just thirty-three.

I received the news from my mother via a telephone call to my bachelor flat, the kennel where I licked my wounds after breaking up with Margaret.

My mother was not crying. She did not sound upset. She

said she would be leaving my father and that she thought I should know first. She could have been giving me a recipe over the phone.

'I am too old for the games of men,' she said.

She already had a new address and phone number, which I wrote down on a small pad. She would 'take up residence' there by late afternoon.

I listened quietly and respectfully. I could see the apartment where she would live, fully furnished, the refrigerator stocked, her favourite chair on the balcony overlooking the harbour. I had a feeling the apartment had been set up for some time – months, possibly years – awaiting her arrival.

'Please join me for dinner Friday evening,' she said.

The blue smoke of my father separated me from my mother. Even in the midst of this upheaval, it wavered between us like a transparent curtain.

'But are you sure?' was all I could say to her.

'I'm sure.'

As she told me the story of my father's infidelity small, familiar detonations went off inside me. I recognised myself. I did not like what I was hearing.

My father had, according to my mother, disappeared to Melbourne for one of his many 'business dealings'. He would be gone for two weeks. There was golf to be played as well. He would not telephone. He never did telephone. My parents were so familiar with each other, so pared back and smooth edged, that they had gone beyond the phoning of each other.

Eleven days into my father's business trip a credit card bill arrived at the family home. It had been a day of gusting winds and heavy rain. Unbeknown to my mother, and least of all my father, the postman had suffered a fall two streets away from our house. The bulk of the contents of his mailbag had spilled onto the footpath sheeted with water, outside the home of my mother's tennis partner, Mrs Betty Pendergast.

By the time the postman had reached my parents' street, the flap of the envelope that contained the credit card bill addressed to my father had eased away from the envelope proper because of its contact with the wet concrete outside the home of Mrs Betty Pendergast.

The envelope was slipped through the mail chute in the front door of the family home just as my mother was reaching for the doorknob on her way out to an Olympics committee meeting of some nature. My mother has always filled her days with tennis and committees.

On retrieving the envelope from the polished floor my mother, an intensely neat and orderly woman, attempted to reattach the curled flap to the envelope. It would not stick.

She thought about the envelope in her hands, and knew that as she drove over the Harbour Bridge towards the restaurant and the committee meeting, as she sipped champagne and sat down to a plate of fresh crayfish, the disorder of the loose flap, the messiness of it, would dog her. She sighed and hurried to the kitchen.

At the table she attempted to dry the envelope with a cloth and had already produced a strip of Cellotape to seal it with when something – she could not say what – drew her to the contents of the credit card bill.

She never read my father's mail. She never inquired as to his whereabouts. She did not know how much he had in the bank. They had become, over the years, like two strangers seated opposite each other in the same train carriage.

But for the first time ever, she looked. And there, two-thirds of the way down the list of items my father had purchased over the past month, was a string of entries that opened a door to my father's second life. When my father was supposed to be holding board meetings in Melbourne, or being taken by limousine through the wineries of the Yarra Valley by clients, he had in fact purchased a box of Romeo y Julieta cigars from Mr Sautter in London. The next item on the statement, beneath the cigars from Mr Sautter, concerned a meal at the Ritz Hotel, also in London. This was, in turn, succeeded by a jewellery purchase from a store in Piccadilly, London.

'That's a long way from Melbourne,' I said to my mother.

'Yes, it is.'

'And it's a long way to go for some Romeo y Julietas.'

'This is not an appropriate time for your humour.'

'I'm sorry, Mother.'

I had a vision of my father buying Romeo y Julietas on the other side of the world when he was supposed to be in Melbourne. I saw him as uncharacteristically cheery, receiving the cigars in the aura of his mistress's perfume. I saw him lighting up, with a vigour that had been lost to most men of his years, after dinner at the Ritz. I could hear the sound of Cara's laughter rising to the ceiling of a suite in the Ritz Hotel with the crisp blue smoke from the Romeo y

Julieta. I could see diamonds twinkling in the dark.

How ironic, I thought, that the smoky tendrils from a cigar could wind their way across continents and into a postman's mailbag and through the chute in the front door of the family home and into the envelope in the hands of my mother.

'Do come Friday,' she said.

'I'll be there.'

I remembered then a brief meeting with my father when I was freshly estranged from Margaret. I had needed – what? To be in the presence of a father's strength, a father's life experience, I think.

I had telephoned him at home.

'Mr Wilson is playing golf,' the maid told me. 'Try calling him on his mobile.'

'Mr Wilson is playing golf,' his mobile message said. It was the maid's voice. I became a trifle confused.

I rang the clubhouse. 'Mr Wilson is playing golf,' the switchboard operator told me.

I decided to leave a message.

Finally, in the early evening, he phoned me.

'I was playing golf,' he said.

'I know.'

'What can I do for you?'

'I thought we could have dinner.'

'Join me tonight,' he said. 'The Jolly Pier, 8 p.m. You know where it is?'

'I know where it is.'

He hung up.

I realised, arriving at the restaurant, that I had not seen

my father for a long time. It goes quickly, time between fathers and sons.

The maître d' took me to the table where my father was engaged in an intimate discussion with a young woman. He was talking into her cleavage, to be precise.

'My son,' he said without standing. 'This is Julie.'

There was something terribly wrong about the table. About the whole scenario.

For one, my father no longer appeared to be my father. He did not look like my father. He did not look like anyone's father.

Gone was the grey short back and sides. He now had a strange bouffant, a lopsided cloud of mustard locks held up, mysteriously, by an invisible gel that had, at some point after application, listed to one side.

Instead of the business suit and tie or his golf clobber he wore a bright red shirt opened to mid-chest, which itself was adorned with a weighty gold chain. I had never known him to wear jewellery of any description, not even his wedding ring.

Then there were the eyebrows. It was these, the eyebrows, that disconcerted me most. Where there had once been extravagant tufts, there were now lean and shaped lines, dyed black as the pelt of a panther. I could barely take my eyes off them.

'Pull up a chair,' he said.

He observed Julie as if she were an exotic plant thought extinct – or more specifically he continued to observe her delicately freckled cleavage – and mumbled something to her through too-moist lips.

'What can I do you for?' he eventually asked.

'Thought we'd catch up.'

'Need money?'

'No.'

'Good. I'm broke. You'd have to ask Julie for a loan.'

The young woman guffawed appreciatively.

'I thought we could have a chat, you know, about a few things.'

'Ask Julie. She does all my talking for me.'

'That's very good, Dad, but I thought we could, well, discuss some things in private.'

'Ask Julie. She does all my privates.'

The young woman roared again and pinched my father's wind-burnt cheek.

'That's very funny, Dad.'

'You're making me feel old, boy, with all the Dad talk.'

He ordered for the three of us and assumed, for a second, his most familiar role – the businessman behind the desk. He wet the tip of a cigar with his lips and looked at me.

'There's a problem here. What is it?'

'I . . . I just need some advice on a few things.'

I felt embarrassed in the presence of Julie. She was too young to even be my father's daughter. I doubt *I* could have chaperoned her without raising some suspicion. And yet she fitted seamlessly in my father's immense orbit. A trinket, to be worn at the Jolly Pier. I looked around the restaurant briefly, and noticed there were several other old men with young companions. I felt I had been caught in some special club of which I was not a member.

'Shoot,' he said, lighting the cigar.

The waiter delivered oysters and I was forced to rise in my seat a little to see over the oyster stand and its silver bowl filled with shaved ice and shells. And when I looked at my father through that damned pall of blue smoke, I immediately forgot why I was there in the restaurant, and what I had wanted to ask.

'It's nothing,' I said.

'Good, let's eat.'

I left quietly after the entrée, on the pretext of having to go to the lavatory, and standing outside the restaurant I watched, for some minutes, the spectacle of my father pressing in on the young and perfumed Julie.

I saw for a moment, the hopelessness of all men. The fear of the ebb and flow of time. The constant reinvention, the shoring up, the barricading against age. The disappearance of a life's experience in the presence of a young female.

Remembering these incidents now, I wonder how many women my father has had over the years. For how long, before the arrival of the envelope, my mother had acted as if his infidelities did not exist, just as wars and poverty and any 'bad news' from the outside world did not exist. I wonder how my father could possibly think his young personal assistants could be sexually interested in him. I wonder if there is something in him that I have inherited, and if that thing was responsible for what happened between Margaret and me.

There was that dinner party with our new neighbour a few years after we were married. There was Jane. There was the brush of her foot up and down my ankle under the dining table. There was that single, brief sexual encounter we shared in her kitchen one afternoon, a year after the night of the steamboat.

Why do we do it? Why do we risk everything for ten minutes of pleasure? What takes us to the edge of destruction?

It was never the same again between Margaret and me. She sensed something. A fracture, undetectable to the eye.

'Is it work, sweetheart?' she asked repeatedly. 'What can I do for you?'

'No, it's not work.'

'When was the last time you had a full check-up with the doctor? I'll make an appointment for you.'

She did, and I was fine. Except for what the doctor could not see. For what only Jane and I knew. Margaret and I never had dinner again at Jane's house. We moved six months after the encounter in her kitchen, precipitating a restlessness that should never have entered our life. We were supposed to be like everyone else. We were supposed to put down roots.

I remember seeing her – Jane – framed by her kitchen window as we did the last of the packing. The ten minutes had been nothing to her. The boiling of a kettle. The washing of a few dishes.

I had become an adulterer. I viewed everything after that through the lens of those 600 seconds. Saw Margaret going about the mechanics of our life and marriage in the context of my unfaithfulness. Everything – Margaret brushing her hair, stepping out of the shower, ironing a shirt, laughing on the telephone – looked different.

As the years moved on this view did not disappear, simply changed and changed again. That brief coupling with Jane, the farce that is stolen sex, meant nothing. I could not remember pressing Jane against the kitchen bench. Could not remember pleasure, if indeed there was any pleasure. But that lame combination of words kept arriving: how could I do it?

And, of course, I did it again.

My mother never moved into her apartment, although I do not doubt she has it still. That she pays the rent dutifully, and keeps the refrigerator stocked, and ensures that the plants are watered. An empty dwelling, a space, that she can go to without ever going to.

She and my father still live in the family home. They keep to their separate bedrooms. They pass each other in the hallway. Two passengers sitting opposite each other in the same train carriage, their faces blank and featureless in the dense smoke from his Romeo y Julieta cigars and her menthol cigarettes.

And I keep remembering one of those few morsels of advice my father ever gave me. 'Never stub your cigar out like a cigarette,' he said. 'It will produce an entirely unpleasant odour. The best way to extinguish a cigar is to let it burn out naturally.'

'That's it?'

'A most beautiful death,' he said.

'Thank you for that, Father.'

'You're welcome,' he said.

TEN

Something French This Way Comes

I SIT here on my favourite stool at the southern end of the Lime Bar and chortle to myself about how nobody knows I have a horse-riding rash the shape of France across my buttocks.

'The drink no good?' Gustave asks.

'Very good, thank you, Gustave.'

'You are okay?'

'*Oui.*'

It is an interesting rash, mapped out by the constant chafe of saddle leather on the long journey down from the Australian Alps.

The trip over, I had hopped into my rented four-wheel drive and headed back to Sydney. I made it as far as Jindabyne before the rash of France imposed itself fully. Sensibly, I checked into a small motel on the lake and slept for seventeen hours.

By the following morning Paris remained troublesome, although the remainder of the rash had eased considerably. I was home by early afternoon.

'You have a joke, is that it?'

'*Non.*'

'You are a very silly man. It is the fresh air that has done this to you.'

'Another gin, lime and tonic, Gustave, and easy on the fresh air.'

'You met some mountain women, eh?'

'Only horses.'

'So you have become unkind also. People cannot help how they are born.'

'I feel an evening of several limes coming on.'

'You are sitting strangely.'

'How rude.'

'You are not sitting as you always sit.'

'You rude barman, you.'

'Perhaps you are still on the horse. Like people who come off a ship and think they are still at sea.'

'Where are you from in France, Gustave?'

'You know where I'm from.'

'Paris, yes?'

'That is a very silly laugh. People with laughs like that can be refused service. It is my right.'

'I see you received my postcard.'

'It was a very silly postcard. You must have been drunk when you bought it.'

'I thought nudists on skis would appeal to a liberal Frenchman such as yourself.'

'It is an insult to the skiing. You know nothing of my culture.'

'I adore France. I am very close to France.'

'But she is not close to you.'

'She is closer than you think.'

'I doubt it.'

'You missed my companionship. That is why you have become a recalcitrant French barman.'

'Your companionship is not missable.'

'I could have you deported.'

'My papers are in order.'

'I will tell the authorities you deal in the illegal trading of limes.'

'My limes are legal.'

'You are a lime pusher with international connections.'

'You are a very silly man.'

'In some countries the pushing of illegal citrus could get you the death penalty.'

'The horses are waiting for you in the mountains.'

'When I win medals in the equestrian events at the Olympics, you will be bragging that you knew me.'

'Please do not tear up the coasters.'

'You used to let me tear up all the coasters I needed to tear up,' I say.

'You sit like there is something lodged in your trousers.'

'Only a recalcitrant French barman would even *look* at my trousers.'

'You are drinking too quickly.'

'It is not my fault you are unable to keep up your illegal supply of limes.'

'You went to the mountains to get yourself together and

you have returned a drunken fool with something in his trousers.'

'You can forget about your tip this evening.'

'You have never remembered.'

'In the mountains I received wisdom.'

'Was that the name of one of your horses?'

'I suppose you think that's funny.'

'Things have been happening here that you could not imagine.'

'I spoke to God in the alps. What could be as enthralling as that?'

'An attractive woman has been asking for you.'

'Let her join the queue.'

'So be it.'

'Who is she?'

'She is in the queue. She is of no interest any longer.'

'Tell me.'

'The queue has snaked around the corner. I can no longer see her.'

'Who?'

'What is a woman in a queue when you have talked to God?'

'I shall find a different use for your limes if you don't tell me immediately.'

'She speaks very good French. We had a lovely conversation.'

'French? A Frenchwoman has been asking after me?'

'As a compatriot I was obliged to tell her everything about you.'

'You must have been talking for hours.'

'About three minutes.'

'Tell me who she is. Tell me, damn you.'

'Please move back from the bar or I shall call security.'

'If you didn't wear glasses I would slap you across the face with my gloves.'

'I don't wear glasses.'

'Then how could you have seen what she looked like?'

'You are very silly. And you have no gloves.'

'I am losing my temper with you.'

'She is coming to dinner.'

'When, tonight?'

'At my home, this Sunday evening.'

'Your home?'

'*Oui*. She has not had the good Provençale home cooking for a while.'

'You are taking home a Frenchwoman who has been asking after me?'

'I did not think you would miss one out of the queue.'

'You are grass-cutting a dear friend?'

'I know not of this grass-cutting. What is grass-cutting? There is no grass to cut.'

'You are stealing this woman away from me?'

'You are very *stupide*.'

'I won't forget this.'

'And I won't forget Sunday night.'

'You are a cad. You are beyond a cad.'

'And I am a very good cook.'

'A cad who cooks dinners for women.'

'I do a wonderful breakfast also.'

'You are cooking my Frenchwoman breakfast?'

'She'll tell me how good it was over lunch.'

'You are no longer my official barman.'

'I shall return the certificate.'

'What time shall I come over on Sunday night?'

'About eight.'

'Shall I bring the wine?'

'Pfffttt. You have gone completely mad.'

'Another lime and tonic, with a splash of gin, Gustave.'

'Of course.'

I can feel my map of France flaring again. But the alcohol, and the thoughts of my future French wife, dull the pain.

ELEVEN

Eiffel, Awful, Earful

ON the morning I awake in the bed of Madame Dubois with a 7-year-old child holding a gun to my head, the first thought I have, funnily, is of an old photograph taken by Henri Cartier-Bresson.

Even Cartier-Bresson probably didn't think of a Cartier-Bresson on first waking. And yet, as a dribble of water from the end of the child's plastic Luger fills my ear, I can see the famous photographer's masked boy on a Paris rooftop.

It is a chilling picture. The subject – a boy of perhaps 12 – is in the middle distance of the picture, which is dominated by angular roof lines and chimneys. He is aiming a gun with steadfast precision at a victim who is out of camera.

What is frightening is that the boy, by accident, by fate, has adopted a stance so familiar these days in newspaper photographs and television footage. It is the classic stance of the unidentifiable terrorist. The boy's *shape* is instantly recognisable.

Cartier-Bresson, genius that he is, has tricked us into

believing, at first viewing, that this is not a boy at all, a child at play, but an adult killer in action. It is only when you study the photograph more closely that you realise it is a harmless scene.

With the Luger in my ear, and the morning light moving across Madame Dubois's creamy European buttocks, I wonder why life often works in reverse to the Cartier-Bresson picture. We stumble into scenes of apparent innocence, like children at play, only to find that they are riddled with menace and ill-intent.

'*Bonjour, mon ami,*' I whisper to the boy. Already I have exhausted my French repertoire.

'Don't move,' he replies.

The child confuses me. I am expecting a rolling, lilting, musical French accent like that of the children in the yoghurt advertisement on television. I expect the sweet innocence of a Notre Dame choirboy. Yet this child's accent is as strongly Australian as a caller's at a country racetrack.

I cannot match the accent with the boy, or what I imagine the boy to be. He holds the plastic Luger steadily with both hands.

I do not wish to risk anything with the boy when it comes to my ears, and in particular my left ear. I have recently suffered my first middle-ear infection, a condition, so my doctor assures me, that is usually the province of children. Initially, I had almost fainted from the pain, and had to take painkillers for over a week to keep it under control. All the while, the sounds that entered the affected ear were so distorted as to be eerie. For a week I had ghosts whistling in my head, whistling at other pretty ghosts, whistling for taxis, whistling the tune of the permanently impaired.

I sigh the sigh of the prisoner about to be executed at dawn, look over at the long, perfect crease line of Madame Dubois's backside, and attempt to clear the fog of Cointreau in my brain, to cut through it, to find a path to the evening before, to dinner at the home of my former barman and confidante, the irascible Gustave.

As my psychiatrist had already concluded, several weeks ago, I am in a phase of intense *sexualus sensitivius* (one of the many ludicrous and persistently annoying invented conditions my therapist expounds to his few clients).

In short, according to him, I was a full-blown case of the tragic impending-divorcee-on-the-lookout-for-any-sexual-possibility. In the shortest of short, my antennae were up.

'It's a common malaise,' my therapist said, picking his teeth.

'You mean a *malaisius commonus*,' I replied.

'*Correctius*.'

'You are very immature for a professional person.'

'Ah!' he said, examining his toothpick. '*Denialus maximus*.' He checked his watch.

'Why don't you *shuttus* your *cakeholius*.'

'Perfectly understandable response for someone with your condition. Same time next week?'

I admit in hindsight, with a child in pyjamas patterned black and white like the hide of a dairy cow, and about to blow out my eardrum with a jet of cold tap water, that I was a trifle manic last night when I first met Madame Dubois at Gustave's.

Again, it was Cartier-Bresson in reverse. I had seen the rooftop boy playing with the toy gun. Not the evil shape of humankind.

'*Bonjouuuur,*' I remember saying to Madame Dubois when she arrived at Gustave's house. I heard Gustave tsk in his most annoying French tsking way.

'May I present Madame Dubois,' he said regally.

'*Enchanté,*' I said, taking her hand and lightly kissing the delicate white skin and blue veins visible beneath it.

Again a tsk from Gustave. I was already drunk. This precipitates one of the symptoms of *sexualis sensitivius*: a tendency to live the experience before anything has happened.

Earlier yesterday I had taken a bottle of chilled gin, a small jug of freshly squeezed lime juice and a bottle of tonic water to the balcony of my flat and basked in the fantasy of meeting the unknown Madame Dubois that evening. She was slender and beautiful. Her hair and eyes were dark. Her skin had the translucence produced only by the pale spring sunshine of Paris.

Before I knew it, it was 6 p.m., half the gin had disappeared, lime pulp clotted the mouth of the jug, the tonic bottle was empty and I was comfortably *drunkus skunkius*. In the space of a few hours I had met this mysterious Frenchwoman, dined with her, made love to her several times and was on a plane to Roissy airport, her hand in mine, her head gently resting against my shoulder, her snore as delicate and heartbreaking as anything ever written by Satie.

I suddenly lost all sense of time. It was not unlike those moments when you awaken and, in half-sleep, study your watch on the bedside table to find it is 1.30 p.m. There is panic. There is a jumping from the bed. There is a general banging into walls. Then, when checking the watch anew, you realise it has been viewed upside down, and it is only 7 a.m.

This was how I was on that Sunday afternoon. I hastily showered and dressed and was at Gustave's place within half an hour.

'You silly man,' he said, standing at the door in his full-length black vinyl chef's apron.

'Sorry if I'm late.'

'You are nearly two hours early.'

'Oh.'

'You have a piece of the shaving cream on your ear lobe.'

'Oh.'

'You are an abomination.'

'May I come in?'

'I do not know why I bother. You are using gin now as the aftershave.'

'Is it that obvious?'

'Pfffttt!' Gustave exclaimed, returning to the kitchen.

I offered to help him with the meal, to stir sauces and chop parsley, but he ignored me. It is one of the beautiful qualities of the French, which I have previously noted with Gustave. They have the ability to make you disappear. I did not exist. Gustave moved around his kitchen as if alone. I retreated to the lounge room.

I snuck a snifter of cognac from Gustave's drinks trolley. I snuck another. And another.

And as I sat nursing my brandy balloon, with the music of Gustave's pot-clanging and whisking and chopping moving around me, I became entranced by the large framed print of Robert Doisneau's famous photograph of the kiss at the Hôtel de Ville.

It was not the lovers I was hypnotised by, that meeting of lips, that clash of teeth, but the rather serious gent passing by in the background. The sturdy, dull, angular and ultimately lonely man whose screaming ordinariness had been captured by the lens of history.

'Oh,' I said unexpectedly, for no reason.

And I knew, then, that I was looking not at a stranger who happened to be passing at the exact moment that the shutter opened and closed, but at myself. At all lonely men on the periphery of life. At all ordinary men on the fringe of something great.

I was filled with an incalculable misery.

'You will suffer moments of sheer, inexplicable despair,' my psychiatrist had warned. 'Much like an aircraft hitting a pocket of air and descending, rapidly, for some seconds.'

'Ah, *flightus interruptus*,' I had said.

'Please do not jest.'

He had been right. There, on the couch at Gustave's place, I momentarily hit my air pocket. I gripped the brandy balloon tightly. I was not ready for Madame Dubois.

As the child continues to push the muzzle of the Luger into my ear, I begin to remember with pleasure the sexual act with

Madame Dubois and take a perverse delight in knowing I have had sex with my assassin's mother. I do not know for sure that this piebald brat is her child, but briefly the thought thrills me.

The more I smile, the harder the child presses the water pistol into my earhole.

'Do not smile,' he says.

When Madame Dubois had finally arrived at the home of Gustave last night, I had come out of the air pocket. I was effusive. I kissed her hand. I spilled red wine on my beige trousers during dinner. I fell in love with her instantly.

Then, at a point where I was beyond comprehending anything pertaining to the moment, to real life, to the world, on account of the gin and cognac and red wine sloshing around in my person like river water in a waterbag attached to the bullbar of a Land Rover, her true purpose in seeking me out was revealed.

'Paperweights?' I asked, nonplussed.

'*Oui*,' she said. 'I hear you are the contact for the Eiffel Tower paperweights in Australia.'

'Eiffel Tower paperweights?'

'*Mais oui*,' she said, somewhat surprised. 'I am in need of 200 for a conference.'

'Conference?'

'On the role of the cheese in modern cuisine.'

'Ah.'

'*Oui*.'

'I understand.'

'*D'accord*!'

How we ended up in bed is unclear. It will come to me. Eventually.

'Don't move,' the boy says.

Then, as I am attempting to unravel the finale of the previous night, the agony and the ecstasy of it, I hear a car pull up in the driveway, below the bedroom window.

The child looks up. He rams the gun into my ear one last time, like all good child assassins, and runs to the window.

'Papa!' he exclaims.

And I freeze as a semi-automatic hand gun goes off somewhere deep inside my head.

TWELVE

The Governor's Pleasure Loses a Client

SINCE I have abandoned alcohol I see, everywhere, things that remind me of alcohol.

Take the city skyline from the balcony of my apartment – a delicious shelf of crystal decanters. The Town Hall clock tower in Balmain – an unopened bottle of Johnny Walker Black Label. The buoys in the harbour – whole fruits bobbing in a giant rum punch. And Centrepoint, through my one good eye – the toothpicked olive in the martini of the city. I like that. I jot it down on an old Lime Bar coaster.

Oh, the pain.

I remember the child brandishing the water pistol in triumph as he saw his dear Papa getting out of the car. I remember Madame Dubois's sleepy, 'Mon petit, what is it?' I remember leaping from the bed and throwing on a shirt and then struggling into my underpants. (Why, in panic, do some men put on shirt and underpants first, and others underpants and trousers?) I remember being unable to locate my trousers as the front door closed downstairs. I remember crawling out the window and onto a ledge as the offensive child assassin poked the butt of his Luger water pistol into *my* butt. I remember dropping from the ledge to the grass below and looking up at a shocked (and tanned) Papa – and into the feeble urination of the child's weapon. I remember being unable to rise, momentarily, on both of my legs, an old tennis injury flaring from the impact of the fall, and tumbling headlong into a soldierly line of mondo grass at the front garden's edge. I remember feeling dazed but struggling to my feet again, the cool of the dew on my naked soles so suddenly soothing, and then a hot, stinging fist to the left eye. A brief, comical wrestle that took out a small plaster garden flamingo at the leg. A dash for the driveway. The explosion of a gnome (in striped shirt and beret) thrown after me. And I remember a brief chase, trouserless, through the narrow back lanes of East Balmain before arriving at the shelter of my apartment block.

My first one-night stand in months and I mishandle it spectacularly, losing a fine (though slightly wine-stained) pair of trousers, a kangaroo-skin belt, Italian loafers, an imitation Tag watch from Hong Kong, skin off my left shin, the sight in one eye and my pride.

'You are okay?' Gustave telephones regularly to check on my condition.

'I'm not doing so good.'

I can hear his distinctive and sarcastic French pfffttt. 'It's been two days, you very silly man.'

'You'll be hearing from my lawyers.'

'I cannot be held responsible for a man who does not have the skill to conduct an affair with a woman for more than one night.'

'I had a gun at my head, if I may remind you.'

'You had a fist in the eye.'

'There was no call for such violence.'

'The fist was attached to the man whose wife you had just slept with.'

'That is no excuse.'

'You were lucky he was French.'

'Yes, you're right, Gustave. It felt like a very French punch.'

'She presented you to her husband, as a challenge.'

'As any overweight Australian businessman would be to some ponytailed French git of a gym instructor.'

'She must do this, now and then. Just as he must have mistresses. It keeps things very much alive.'

'And made me very nearly dead.'

'You were sacrificed, my friend.'

'I thought she wanted my Eiffel Tower paperweights.'

'You were the sad little *coq* brought to the boiling *vin*.'

'Oh, please. I refuse to speak to you any longer. Can you ever talk without mentioning booze? Go away.'

'Did you know, from my attic, your block of flats looks like a giant bottle of Cointreau . . .'

'I'm hanging up.'

As I nurse the bag of Edgell's frozen peas on my swollen left eye, I know alcohol is at the core of not just my embarrassing fracas with the Frenchwoman's husband, but all the problems and inconsistencies in many other areas of my life.

'You must relearn the rules of the affair,' Gustave tells me the next time he rings.

'I don't want to speak to you.'

'Always co-join on neutral territory.'

'*Cojones*?'

'*Non*, co-join.'

'I have developed a massive distaste for the French accent.'

'If you must give a phone number, make it your mobile.'

'I don't own a mobile. They give you tumours.'

'You must have a mobile if you are to conduct an affair.'

'Do you have a mobile?'

'I have three mobiles.'

'I'm hanging up now.'

I try to rid my mind of Gustave's rules for affairs. It is not difficult. My thoughts return, instantly, to alcohol.

The telephone rings again.

'I bet they're all analog, aren't they, you cheap French barman.'

'Pardon?'

'Hello?'

It is my friend Neil from the squash club.

'Just reminding you it's the Governor's Pleasure tomorrow.'

'It's Governor's Pleasure time already?'

'Afraid so.'

It strikes me, on the line to Neil, that the encounter with the fist of a jealous French husband has, in fact, been more than an encounter with the fist of a jealous French husband. It has proved to be, as they like to say now, a 'wake-up call'.

Gustave is right. I know nothing of the rules of behaviour. Of life. And lately I have forgotten all the rules of alcohol.

'I'm sorry, Neil,' I say, 'I shall have to pass.'

I place the telephone in its cradle before he can object. I am, at least, becoming adept at hanging up the telephone.

I try to imagine the impact of my rejection of Neil and a place at our regular luncheon table in the Governor's Pleasure restaurant.

A varying group of us have been dining there for over a year. There are the core club members – myself, Neil, his retired disc-jockey neighbour and a tobacco importer known to us all – and a string of guests invited only after a full committee vote.

The restaurant is a windowless basement beneath a bank in the city, furnished with art-deco mirrors and the world's smallest catwalk replete with brass pole. Around the tongue of the miniature stage are the tables. Ours is always reserved, at the end of the catwalk, for the first Monday of the month.

For a significant sum the luncheon consists of an entrée and main course, several beers, wine, three strippers, dessert personally served by the dancer of your choice (as schoolgirl, French maid, et cetera), and cigars, followed by a lurch up the spiral staircase to the exit, and an astonished arrival into mid-evening. How often we have swayed there on the footpath, unable to speak, stunned at the loss of the sun.

I always, of course, scuttle to the comfort of the Lime Bar, where I regale Gustave with descriptions of young, naked women. Then I become melancholy. All I can think of, with some sadness, is the person who comes out from behind the curtains in the Governor's Pleasure and sprays and wipes the brass pole, between dancers. I always wonder: as a job, how do you describe that?

Neil, on the other hand, always shares the taxi with me in good faith but passes out just after the Anzac Bridge. I then reach into his suit-jacket pocket, pull out the preprepared tag with his address printed on it and pin it to his lapel.

The retired disc jockey, I am told, always walks directly to his former offices in the city and is ejected by the security guards.

'Just habit, I suppose,' Neil says.

And the tobacco importer returns to his huge housing complex on the shores of Hen and Chicken Bay and without fail gets lost in its labyrinth. On several occasions he has wandered into the wrong flat, on the wrong floor, in the wrong tower, and caused mayhem.

'He's that sort of chap,' Neil says. 'He'll try any doorknob once.'

I think of all the sad and sorry figures who are now my friends and how, in life, your friends of the moment truly reflect your moment. How they mirror your own state of mind: your fears and desires, your strengths and weaknesses.

I take the bag of peas from my eye and telephone Gustave.

'Who?'

'You know who it is.'

'*Ah oui*. They are talking about you all over town.'

'They? What are they saying?'

'They are saying a man was robbed of his trousers by a child who held a gun to his buttocks.'

'Very funny.'

'They are saying this man then assaulted the fist of a French gym instructor with his eye and fled.'

'Ha ha.'

'They are saying the police have an artist's impression of this buttocks.'

'Gustave . . .'

'And that capture is imminent.'

'This is not funny any more.'

'You are boring when you don't drink.'

'Thank you.'

'I think we can no longer be friends. Now that you have given up drinking.'

'Don't say that, Gustave.'

'It is a rule of being French.'

'I need your help.'

'We have been down this path before.'

'Seriously, Gustave. I need . . . I need to learn how to live again.'

I can hear the long sigh of Gustave down the line.

'Perhaps,' he says.

'Oh, thank you, Gustave.'

'Maybe.'

I can also hear a high-pitched robotic rendition of the French national anthem being played.

'It is one of my mobiles,' Gustave says. 'We shall speak soon.'

Already I feel confident. That I will break this crazy, destructive pattern of behaviour. That I will, once more, catch up with my own age.

Are we ever our own age? What age are we at any given time? How, in my mid-forties, can I be thinking and behaving like a teenager? No, that is inaccurate. I am behaving worse than a teenager. Having accrued at least some wisdom, albeit accidentally, with the passage of forty-five years, to behave as I am behaving is shameful. Then how do you act maturely? Is to be inoffensive mature? Is to live life according to other people's civilised expectations mature? I will become mature, I think. I will cloak myself in maturity.

And yet I know, even as I think this, that a part of me is still there in the darkness, watching the small figure buff and polish the brass pole, and anticipating the arrival of the next naked figure on the world's smallest stage.

THIRTEEN

Delicates: Hand Wash Only

GUSTAVE tells me I had probably learned the rules of living from my parents by the age of five.

Anything that came after that, he says, has been my own perverted attempt to rebel against their strictures. Gustave says that for many of us, our lives are nothing but an unending battle against the 'template of the parent'.

'You are speaking from the perspective of a man whose country of birth is by nature rebellious,' I say defiantly.

'You see,' he says, 'you are rebelling against my claim of your rebelliousness. I cannot continue when you are in this frame of mind. If you wish to pick up the balls and leave the playground, then so be it.'

'What balls?'

'Still you fight me.'

'Which playground?'

'Have you always been like this?'

'Like how?'

'So – how you say? – brattish.'

'You are telling me I learned everything about the rules of life by the time I was 5 years old?'

'Correct.'

'And that I have since chosen to, shall I say, muddy this parental knowledge?'

'That is what I am alleging.'

'Alleging. Now you're alleging. I could be in the presence of some hokey relieving magistrate, in a makeshift court in a tiny, nondescript village of idiots and inbreds in a remote corner of the Loire Valley, with all your alleging.'

'The Loire Valley has no corners.'

'Everywhere has a corner.'

'But this is a court, that is true.'

'Ah.'

'You have asked me to judge the way you live, to expose your distorted – is that the word, distorted? – rules of living, and advise you accordingly.'

'That is correct, your worship.'

'Then we shall have to start at the beginning.'

'Now we're getting somewhere.'

'By the way, what is hokey?'

'Gustave, do you really want to know what my parents taught me up to the age of five?'

'Please, please, I am the ear here. Commence.'

'By 5 I knew that bourbon went with ginger ale. I knew that food was often consumed in restaurants, not at home. I knew that when mothers cried and threw crockery and tossed your father's underwear and pyjamas onto the front lawn, they received diamonds. I knew that when fathers dressed in their golfing outfits they didn't come home until after midnight. I knew that Christmas Day was the saddest day of the year: that friendship could be obtained instantly with the exchange of gifts. I knew that the smell of cigar smoke meant your father was home. I knew that the absence of cigarette smoke meant your mother had gone out. I knew —'

'Please, you are giving me too much at once. It is too heartbreaking,' says Gustave.

'It is what you would expect from a child who was given an executive briefcase for his first day at school.'

'But you became an executive, *monsieur*. Of sorts. An executive of the paperweights.'

'That is my point.'

'Please, I am not the analyst.'

'You are the finest analyst I have ever known.'

'I cut limes for a living.'

'Many lime cutters have made great analysts.'

'You are doing this deliberately,' Gustave says, 'to steer away from the matter at hand.'

'I am thinking of the matter at hand. My hand would like a drink.'

'We cannot drink when we are discussing the rules of life.'

'People only ever discuss the rules of life when they drink. Surely, as a barman, you would have learned that by now.'

'They are different rules, those rules,' Gustave says. 'People discuss how they *want* to live their lives, not how they actually must.'

'If I had a drink I would agree with you. Please, Gustave, don't make me beg.'

'This is one of the rules I wish to discuss. I think you drink too much, and for the wrong reasons.'

'I drink because it makes me feel good.'

'You are repeating what you have heard your father say, when you were five.'

'That is not true. You would not want to hear what my father has to say about drink.'

'Tell me,' says Gustave.

'I would need a drink to tell you.'

'This is a complicated cycle.'

'Never drink and cycle.'

'That is a joke?'

'Yes.'

'You need some new jokes.'

'I'm funnier when I drink.'

'In France we have a reason to drink.'

'Being French will do that to you.'

'We drink to complement the meal. We drink to consolidate friendship. We drink for the digestions.'

'You drink quite a lot.'

'You are missing my point. Your drinking has no sensible purpose. It is to hide from the pain.'

'Now I have pain?'

'Yes, you have pain,' Gustave says. 'You are drinking to obliterate the wife that was.'

'It's cheaper than paying a hitman. No. That's incorrect. Not in the long run.'

'You are an idiot sometimes, excuse me.'

'I am waiting to hear your rules of life, as you promised. I'm not paying good money for this for nothing.'

'I am doing this for free, you know that.'

'Barmen never give you anything for free.'

'We are wasting our time,' Gustave says.

'I'm sorry. Okay. Let's be serious. Gustave, tell me what's wrong with me?' I open my arms wide, to stress the point.

'If you ever had rails, you have gone off them, as I see it.'

'Rails?'

'Correct. You are unsure about yourself. You have no confidence since it punctured between you and Margaret.'

'Punctured?'

'*Oui.*'

'What do you know about Margaret and me? How can you know more than me about Margaret and me when even I'm not sure about Margaret and me?'

'Please do not distract.'

'Punctured?'

'Yes. You are crying out for love and yet you feel unworthy of love. Because of the Margaret puncture. So you are drinking, to try and build the confidence that you have lost. You drink and drink. Then, when you are drunk, you look for the love. You are too delicate to do this. You are the hand wash only at this stage. This is a disaster.'

'A disaster.'

'We shall not go into the evening with my French friend.'

'No, we shall not.'

'Don't you see, then? Don't you see what is happening?'

'I know I should have had creamed rice as a child. Like the other kids did.'

'Please, don't regress so quickly. The rules of life are no – how do you say? – quick shopping list.'

'And they had those sandwiches with the hundreds and thousands in them . . .'

'Please.'

'All I had were leftover prunes wrapped in bacon, and cocktail onions.'

'No more, please.'

'How I've hated cocktail onions all my life.'

'The point is this: you cannot wash away the pain of the puncture with alcohol. It is impossible.'

'I've given it a darned good shake.'

'You have shaken it, yes. But it is still there, no?'

'Yes.'

'Good,' says Gustave. 'At last we are getting somewhere.'

'I don't know what to do. I see Margaret more now, in my mind, than I did when we were married.'

'*Oui*,' says Gustave, nodding. 'It is the way.'

'And the limes, Gustave. The limes. The smell of them. The citrus. It was there, in her perfume, that citrus smell.'

'*Oui, oui*. I know this.'

'You know about Margaret's perfume?'

'From what you say, *monsieur*, she seems the citrusy type of woman.'

'I wonder all the time where she is, Gustave. Where she is living. Who she is seeing. I have followed couples, women who I thought were Margaret.'

'*Monsieur*, she is safe and not with the attachment. You must not concern yourself with this.'

He looks at me briefly – is there a trace of panic in his face? – then begins busily polishing the bar top.

'How do you know that, Gustave?'

'I know not, *monsieur*. It is my instinct about these things. About the women. I'm French, *oui*? Anyway, it is okay. Cry if you want to. The crying is okay.'

'Tell me what to do. What? Do I go onto light beers? I hate light beers. They taste like soap.'

'Forget about the beers.'

'Shandies. Who drinks shandies nowadays? Grand-mothers. Very old grandmothers, they drink shandies.'

'You are defining everything by the alcohol. I am beginning to think our friendship is not what you need.'

'I need it, Gustave.'

'That I am a barman, and you define everything by the alcohol.'

'You could change jobs.'

'Your jokes are improving.'

'Thank you.'

'I cannot stop you from drinking. You are a grown man.'

'Yes, I'm a grown man. Aren't I?'

'But I can refuse to serve you, as a personal protest.'

'That would be against your sworn oath as a barman.'

'Please, stop the jokes. I am being serious with you. It is the alcohol. Only without the binge can we start to rebuild you.'

'I like the sound of that.'

'Very well.'

'Very well.'

'We start now. You will be my Mrs Dolittle,' Gustave says.

'You've lost me.'

'I shall teach you to rain in Spain, on the plain.'

'I'm ready.'

'*Bon.*'

'Let's have a drink. To celebrate,' I say, excited.

FOURTEEN

The Little Goat Shepherd
of Nebraska

I HAVE been banned from the Lime Bar.

After several private meetings with my barman and friend Gustave who, in his inimitable manner, attempted to repair what he calls the *débâcle* of the *train de marchandises* that is my life, I disappointed him so bitterly that he imposed a two-month refusal of entry on me.

Naturally I protested vehemently.

I told him that he was legally unable to do so unless I had perpetrated unacceptable behaviour within the province of the Lime Bar. I reminded him that entry could only be barred if I had committed an act offensive to the code of conduct of the bar, or to other patrons, or to bar staff specifically.

'Bull,' he said.

In a formal letter of protest I reminded him that no allegations had been levelled against me in regard to my behaviour within the province of the Lime Bar, and that as a regular citizen it was my right to enter and leave at whatever time it pleased me.

'*Décombres*!' he said, snorting over the phone.

I further threatened to take him and the Lime Bar management not only to the Equal Opportunities Board, but also to the governing body overseeing all such public houses, to state my case of unreasonable banishment, and that a damages claim would be issued forthwith.

In return I received a letter from Gustave on Lime Bar stationery, which said succinctly, 'Grow up.'

As a result, I have taken my business to the nearby downstairs bar of the Vesuvio Restaurant. It is small – a pretend bar for the pre-dinner drinks of restaurant diners – and I quickly discover that I am the only regular.

It is here that I draft further letters to Gustave and various governmental and humanitarian bodies. And I am tolerated by the Vesuvio because, I think, they assume I am a serious and somewhat important restaurant critic who is, judging by my regular patronage of both bar and restaurant, assessing the Vesuvio for a hatted place in the latest city restaurant guide. That I am here so often indicates I must be teetering between two hats and three. I notice, after several appearances, that they repeatedly play Joe Cocker's 'You Can Leave Your Hat On' over heavily bassed speakers.

Free drinks have started to come my way.

Still, I have not been able to hide my longing for the familiar surrounds of the Lime Bar, so after ten days I have decided to confront Gustave in an attempt at reconciliation.

It is late on Saturday evening and I find him placing rubbish in the alley behind the bar.

'Gustave, it is me,' I say, standing in the half-darkness.

'Ah,' he says, without looking up. 'Where else do the rats wait but in the alleyway?'

'Please, Gustave.'

'You have been banned.'

'From the alley?'

'You have broken your parole.'

'I'm in an alley for Chrissake.'

'You are within 2 metres of Lime Bar property.'

'The garbage?'

'The property of the bar all the same. Be off with you.'

'I was always told the French were cruel.'

'I have better things to do than talk to you. I have toilets to clean.'

'Gustave, my friend.'

'You have the wrong Gustave.'

'There is only one Gustave.'

'Who are you?'

'I'm sorry I let you down, Gustave.'

I move closer to him, into the glow of light.

'The wolf at the edge of the firelight shows his face,' he says.

'Please, Gustave, no more sayings.'

'I cannot help you any more. I do not think it is wise for you to have a friend who is a barman any longer.'

'Please speak to me for just a moment . . .'

'I hear you have gone into the restaurant critic business.'

'That's not true.'

'Waiters are losing sleep all over town.'

'Let me come back, Gustave.'

'As they say on *Oprah*,' he says, with finality, 'you are responsible for your own unhappiness.'

I think about this on the walk back to my flat, and then become cranky with Gustave for quoting *Oprah* and making me think about it so much. I wish, momentarily, I was as smart as Oprah, and could earn millions of dollars each week simply conducting my own televisual autobiography year after year. I wish I was so powerful I could criticise a cut of beef and send the entire United States meat industry into crisis. I wish I had been brought up in poverty and had had to make my own school shoes out of cardboard fruit cartons and twine, and eat 'bread and iffit', whatever that was, day and night, and sleep head to toe with seven brothers and sisters on one side of a single bed, with my parents, also head to toe, on the other half, and that my father worked in a coal mine and hacked and spluttered whilst, still wearing a dirty under-shirt, he washed himself in a tin tub in front of a small fire of flickering coal pieces collected by myself from the slag pits after school, and that the entire family's heads were shaved because of lice and people hollered abuse at us across the street – 'The bowling-ball family! The bowling-ball family!' – and that I was one day noticed by a diligent and infinitely understanding teacher who took me under her or his wing, having recognised my entrepreneurial genius, and managed to steer me out of the poverty cycle, despite my obvious poverty-induced anger and recalcitrant nature, and allowed me to develop my own ideas, namely screenprinting T-shirts with slogans that reflected my anger and recalcitrant nature, namely 'Rack Off', and other such expressions, and that I made money from this and then the next business and the next business until I was head of an international chain of fast food outlets called Iffit, and eventually a movie was made about the special relationship between myself and my teacher and I progressed to having my own chat show where all I had to say was that I liked a particular book, for example, even though it happened to be the greatest bag of saccharine and nonsense and drivel, and immediately ten million people would buy the aforementioned book and I would alleviate other people's poverty in an instant. I also wish I could tell my huge audience that limes are carcinogenic and get Gustave to lose his job.

But Gustave (or Oprah) is right. I am responsible for my own well-being. I have derailed myself and blamed everyone else for it.

As it turns out, fate delivers a solution.

It is during my fortnightly rub-down from my masseur, Kenneth, that I first learn of the imminent arrival of the American motivationalist Marty Powers.

Ordinarily, I don't listen to anything Kenneth says during the rub-down. Ordinarily, the only thing we discuss is the relaxation tape of my choice at the beginning of the session. Ordinarily, I choose the deep-in-the-Amazon tape, which, with its cacophony of macaws and monkeys, its trickling streams and the occasional distant mumbles from some lost yet extremely relaxed pygmy tribe, usually precludes any opportunity for Kenneth to interject. The death cries of a macaw being roasted alive over a pygmy child's camp fire is far preferable to Kenneth's inane babble.

On this occasion, however, Kenneth has vital news to impart. He has secured gold passes for himself and his mother to a one-day motivational camp to be held by the guru Marty Powers.

I have never heard of Marty Powers and am more concerned, as always, with Kenneth's habit of inching the white towel down over my buttocks as he kneads away at my body like an award-winning French pastry chef. I have had my doubts about Kenneth since the moment he told me his name was Kenneth. It is a name that seems to lack the sinew and stamina of a legitimate masseur.

Nevertheless, he tells me that Marty Powers is the guru of all gurus in the motivation world, a calibre above even the great Anthony Robbins. Kenneth and his mother have also attended an Anthony Robbins camp. It left Kenneth cold, he said, although his mother, post-Robbins, has fulfilled her dream of heading up a Latin American dance school, and is also running a very lucrative sideline in prosthetic fruits, thank you very much.

Kenneth explains that the hot-coal-walking component of the motivational camp turned him against Robbins. I find this, as an exercise in motivation, quite perplexing. I figure it would only come in handy if I ever accidentally knocked over the backyard Webber, set my pants on fire, and had to negotiate the spilled coals to reach the hose. Kenneth happened to burn the soles of his feet. But it motivated him, at least, to attend a first-aid class.

Kenneth says it was Mr Robbins's famous book *Awaken the Giant Within* that alerted him to the possibilities that life offered. As I listen to the wistful chattering of monkeys mating, flea-checking each other's coats and doing the usual array of disgusting things that monkeys do to each other in the forest, I think what a marvellous concept that is. That a giant resides in all of us. I think I would like to write a weight-loss book called *Reduce the Giant Within*. I think that awakening the giant would surely cause practical problems. How, when the giant is awoken, does it get out? Via which route does the giant exit? I blame the filthy monkeys on the relaxation tape for my thinking about the horrible anatomical consequences.

Still, Kenneth has tweaked my interest (and my backside, once again, mind you, near the end of the session, but that's another story). On my way home I drop into my local book-store and purchase Marty Powers's latest masterpiece, his international bestselling fable *The Little Goat Shepherd of Nebraska*. I decide to read it in one sitting.

Unbelievably, by the first page Powers has me doubting my own intelligence. I was completely unaware that they had goat shepherds in Nebraska. I begin to feel very unso-phisticated and novice-like in Powers's hands.

Then the story takes hold of me. One day the little goat shepherd wakes to attend to his flock (are there 'flocks' of goats? I decide to trust the eloquent Powers) and finds that his entire family – Mammy, Pappy and thirteen sisters – have been struck dead by a series of freakishly clustered lightning bolts.

I don't pause to ask what the little goat shepherd's parents and thirteen sisters were doing wandering a neighbouring field prior to 5 a.m. as the worst storm in the history of Nebraska passed overhead. I know it will be explained later.

Nevertheless, as the little goat shepherd surveys the wretched scene – the bodies, quote, 'resting as tangle-limbed and disarrayed as porcelain-faced dolls thrown into the air by some mad, schizophrenic dollmaker bereft of medication', unquote – he realises, at that moment, that death is but a part of life, and that his destiny is now in his own tiny hands.

I get quite tearful at this point in the fable, as the little goat shepherd is left to bury his family, one by one, in the family plot out back of the farmhouse. There, amidst the graves of his Civil-War-veteran Grandpappy and his long-suffering Grandmammy – who, on the sudden death of Grandpappy, built her own covered wagon single-handedly and transported not just Grandpappy's bullet-ravaged body but a family of several dozen children, housemaids and farm hands to the serenity of Nebraska all those years ago – the little goat shepherd shovels for an eternity. Then he works on the wooden crosses in his Pappy's toolshed and lovingly carves inscriptions from the Bible on each. Following a brief final ceremony, during which the little shepherd and several hundred goats stand silently and in reverence around the line of graves, the boy packs a small checked tablecloth full of his worldly belongings, attaches it to a stick, and heads out towards the horizon, quote, 'to the mystical tinkling of goat bells', unquote.

Taking a well-needed breather from the book, I wish, for a moment, I had the courage of the little goat shepherd. I return eagerly to the fable.

The boy suffers all the hardships of travel (he is, after all, only 4 years old), but he is nurtured and cared for by his devoted flock of goats. At night, as cold winds sweep across the Midwest plains, the goats take it in turns to assemble themselves in a pyramid formation, much like a stack of gymnasts, to form a rudimentary shelter for the young prophet. In the evening, as the boy sleeps, the winds of the plains sound the goats' bells like ancient Tibetan chimes.

Living on goat's milk and goat's cheese, the boy travels from town to town spreading his message about life and death and the dangers of lightning.

'Not even in thine own field is one safe from the fork of fate,' says the boy. 'Wherever thou be, death is but a thunder-clap away. So rejoice in thy life, and the life of others, and spread love and goodness, preferably indoors in the advent of a thunderstorm.'

The little goat shepherd's words leave a trail of warmth and goodwill that affects everyone around him. And just as his several hundred goats exude the sweet aroma of farm-yard manure, so the little goat shepherd's good tidings linger in the air.

All along the way the little goat shepherd meets ignorance and skepticism.

'What are you trying to say?' asks one town drunk, spit-ting tobacco from the corner of his mouth. (I am furious with the old wino, so caught up in the story am I.)

'I am saying,' replies the little goat shepherd, 'that myself and my beloved goats do not know where we will be or what we will encounter, from one hour to the next.

And yet, ultimately, it all forms the pattern of a life in the end. Thus are the implicit vagaries yet sustainable unpredictabilities of a life less ordinary.'

I am thoroughly impressed by the 4-year-old's use of the phrase 'sustainable unpredictabilities'. I think back to my own vocabulary at his age and conclude that child prophets seem to have unlimited mature dialogue at their disposal.

The boy takes pity on the wino, and instructs him on the meaning of life, and manages, such is the power of his influence, to wean him off his poisonous vices. The bum instantly denounces alcohol, swears off chewing tobacco and, as we learn in a footnote, becomes the premier advocate of the virtues of goat's milk and goat's cheese in the entire Midwest. Powers informs us, also, that the pitiful wino not only promotes the benefits of healthy and natural living, but starts a health-food chain that, in less than fifty years, becomes one of the biggest naturopathic retail outlets in the United States. In the touching footnote, Powers quotes the former wino in his dotage, sitting in a rocking chair on the balcony of his ranch-style summer villa in Monaco: 'If it weren't for that young'un and his goaties . . .'

Finally, the little goat shepherd reaches the ocean. (The geography of the book is unclear. I thought he was heading towards Canada, but this is a trifle, and does not undermine the strength and beauty of the fable.) And there, as his hundreds of goat companions trot down and stand with him at the water's edge, their little hooves sinking ever so slightly into the sand, he witnesses a most spectacular dawn.

At this, the goats begin to sing a celestial hymn. It is a

hymn to the beauty of the world and all the creatures in it. It is a hymn so all-pervading and glorious that even the fish in the sea can hear it, and the rocks and the clouds and the palm trees. Even members of the Cambridge Boys' Choir on the other side of the world hear it and learn new musical phrasings and harmony structures from the supernatural croonings of the goats.

Then, out of nowhere, clouds rush across the sky and form the exact faces of the little goat shepherd's lost parents and sisters. And there's Grandmammy, smiling at him as she fixes another steel tread to a broken wagon wheel. And there's Grandpappy, his bearded face as stern and yet as compassionate as ever, even though half of his forehead has been blown off by a Confederate musket ball. And all of them join in with the hymn-singing goats, so that all the people of the world can hear this heavenly tune.

Then, in the fable's penultimate moment, the goats, still singing, and yet in a trance, resume their gymnastic positions and form a giant, teetering, towering pyramid. The little goat shepherd climbs and climbs up the side of this goat scaffolding and, finally, stands atop the tall animal structure and opens his arms.

'Reach for the sky!' he shouts, accompanied by the goats' singing and the tinkling of several hundred bells and the sudden, glorious outbreak of the dawn sun, the beams flooding over the boy until he disappears.

I am left weeping at the end of the book. 'Reach for the sky!' I shout through my tears. It takes me some time to recover.

When I finally do, I manage to find out through my contacts that Marty Powers is staying in the Michael Parkinson Suite at the Sebel Townhouse in Sydney.

I get into my car straight away and drive to the hotel, my moist-paged copy of *The Little Goat Shepherd of Nebraska* sitting on the passenger's seat.

'Reach for the sky!' I shout, punching the air, and a hole in the vinyl roof of my convertible.

FIFTEEN

Power to the Purple

I FEEL something of a fraud sitting in the bar of the Sebel of Sydney, waiting for an audience with the American motivationalist, guru and bestselling author Marty Powers.

It has been two hours since I first asked the concierge to relay a message to the great Powers, and I am the only one in the dimly lit bar, clutching my copy of his fable *The Little Goat Shepherd of Nebraska* and surrounded by photographs of the famous people who have stayed at the Sebel.

The barman is pretending to work. He is washing and polishing already clean glasses, rearranging the liquor bottles on the shelf and repeatedly glancing at me. He has obviously seen anxious fans before. It may also have something to do with the fact that I have yet to order anything.

When he starts dispensing salted nuts and little curried snacks in bowls, I feel compelled to buy a drink.

'A gin, lime and tonic, please,' I say through the dimness, and his sigh is audible.

He is one of those annoying barmen who affects, indeed

exaggerates, his foreignness. He calls everyone 'guv', which I find exceedingly annoying from the outset. It is reverse-condescension condescension. It is an affectation that Gustave, thankfully, has never adopted. Perhaps because it is so difficult to pretend to be French. Either you are French or you are not. There are no guvs in France.

As he mixes my drink with careless haste, and cuts the lime in a slovenly manner – my glass eventually contains a single misshapen wedge and I can't help but think that Gustave would have been appalled – the concierge approaches with a message.

'Mr Powers will be with you shortly,' he says, and leaves.

I go cold with excitement and nerves. I take another sip of my drink and glance down at the cover of his book. Despite the poor lighting I can still make out the impression-istic painting of the little goat shepherd, teetering atop his pyramid of goats, his arms extended to the rising sun, and a warmth rushes through me.

I am suddenly feeling more confident, and the pictures of Danny La Rue and Ricky May and other tremendous celebrities on the walls of the bar no longer intimidate.

'The lime,' I say to the barman, 'could be a touch more artful.'

He stares at me, incredulous. 'Beg your pardon, guv?'

'Your lime work could do with a bit of, well, work.'

It is as if the mere proximity of Powers has infused me with a preternatural sureness, an understanding of the Big and Small things in life.

I chuckle to myself. I recall the last time I was here, in the

Sebel, with my old yachting chum Eddy. It is the sort of bar that induces confession. I cannot be sure if it's the décor, or the very architecture of the room, but every time I have attended the Sebel I have either been confided in or confided to someone. Perhaps it's just because everyone in the Sebel, at any given time, is drunk.

For example, I had never known, until our evening in the Sebel, that there were in fact two Eddys.

'Please don't tell anyone,' he whispered in a Brazil-nut breath, 'but most days, when I'm confident, that's Big Eddy going out into the world. When I'm more vulnerable, however, and perhaps a little down on myself, then I'm Little Eddy.'

Poor Eddy. I vow here and now to send him a copy of *The Little Goat Shepherd of Nebraska*. (But know, instinctively, he will ask whether there is a companion volume; namely, *The Big Goat Shepherd of Nebraska*.)

And that is when Marty Powers walks in.

I am instantly taken aback by his smallness of frame. He is as slender as a boy, and dressed immaculately in skin-tight black denim jeans and a black shirt buttoned at the cuffs. He wears Cuban-heeled boots with elaborate white stitching around the toes. His large oval belt buckle is as big as a soap dish. His hair is a brilliant silver and as he turns his head, looking around in the gloom, I notice the silhouette of an immaculately plaited ponytail.

I stand. 'Mr Powers?'

'Well, hello,' he says, striding over. 'Darn hard to see yer there, my friend.'

He shakes hands. It is a strong grip. A cattle rancher's grip. For a moment James Dean in *Giant* flashes across my mind. Marty Powers sits beside me at the bar.

'Thank you for your time.'

'Well, my pleeesure, friend,' he says. 'It's not often I get a fan so well versed in my leeterary endeavours.'

He cannot see my flush of embarrassment. On my arrival I had immediately found the Michael Parkinson Suite where he was staying and read at length from *The Little Goat Shepherd of Nebraska* outside his door, before being quietly removed by the concierge. I thought, as a master of motivation and life goals, he would appreciate the initiative.

'It is indeed an honour,' I say.

'Gin martini with a twerst,' he shouts over his shoulder. 'Now, sir, how may I be of assistance?'

I do not answer him straight away. How can I tell him I am looking for meaning in my life? That somehow I have slipped my moorings, and am drifting out to sea? That I am a failure in romance? That not even the most sophisticated French barman on the east coast of Australia can set things right?

'I was very moved,' I say hesitantly, 'by your fable.'

'Why thank yer,' he says. I marvel at how Marty Powers manages to talk through his smile. Nothing moves. The upturned crescent of his mouth is fixed.

'It was,' I say, 'like nothing I have ever read.'

'Friend, I am indeed grateful. Y're too kind. Now, how may I be of assistance?' I can see him checking his Rolex.

'I just wanted to say thank you.'

'Well no, let me thank *yer*, my friend.'

'No, thank *you*.'

He drinks his martini straight down. It seems to relax him. He settles on his stool.

'Let me tell yer the seengular most satisfyin' moment of my life,' he says. 'I fly all aroun' the world, and one day I was walkin' through a shopping mall in London. That's London, England, my friend. And I hears a little girl talkin' to her mama about the little goat shepherd of Nebraska. I'm thinkin', here I am over in London, England, and a little darlin' is talking to her mama about the little goat shepherd. And yer know what I do? I go right on up to her and I say, "That's me, darlin'. I'm the man who writ the story of the little goat shepherd." And she can't believe it, she thinks I'm some sorta crazy man.' He lets off a shotgun laugh. 'Another martini, friend,' he shouts over his shoulder. 'Gin, with a twerst. And then,' he continues to me, 'I take a copy of that little ole book out of my briefcase and show her my photeegraph on the back cover and I say, "See, darlin'? That's me. Marty Powers." And still she don't believe me. That, my friend, was one of the happiest moments I ever had.'

He again takes his drink in a single swallow and smacks his lips. 'I ain't famous, my friend. It's my story. It's the little goat shepherd. It's his message that has travelled aroun' the world and changed so many people's larves.'

'I know how the little girl feels,' I say.

'Let me tell yer something, my friend. The one thing I

know in this larf, we's all little children at heart. We all have the little goat shepherd in us.'

I have been so enraptured by his insights that I have failed to notice until now that a young woman has arrived at the bar. I look to see if Marty Powers has seen her, and he is already staring in her direction.

'Excuse me one moment, my friend,' he says, and he is there, instantly, beside her, leaning against the bar as if it were just another fence post on his private one-million-hectare cattle ranch in Texas.

I do not have to strain to hear him talk. He has a voice that seems to reach every corner of the room.

'Well, little darlin',' he is saying. 'Sometimes yer just got to follow yo' personal journey.'

I like that. I make a mental note of it. Personal journey.

'That little butterfly clip in yo' hayir,' he adds. 'That's very good luck, my darlin'. If Marty Powers has a moteef, it's that pretty little butterfly. Best to live beautifully for a short time, I always say, and flutter on that wind.'

I sit on my own for up to half an hour as he motivates the young woman. I now know one of the secrets of Marty Powers's success – he loves people.

Eventually he comes over to me, the woman on his arm.

'My friend, it was indeed a pleeesure,' he says. 'But a personal journey takes me elsewhere.'

'Of course,' I say.

Without asking, he picks up my copy of *The Little Goat Shepherd of Nebraska* and signs it with a rudimentary, child-like drawing of a butterfly.

'All power to yer,' he says, winking, and leaves the bar with the woman.

I am too exhilarated to move, to finish my drink, to do anything. I am filled to the brim with thoughts of my own personal journey and butterflies and goats and the dazzle of Marty Powers's smile.

I leave the bar and wait in the foyer on a couch next to a giant 2-metre-tall stuffed teddy bear soon to be auctioned for a children's charity, or so the sign pinned to the bear's belly says. I have decided to catch one last glimpse of Marty Powers, on his way to his lecture at the Town Hall.

Just after 8 o'clock he emerges from the lift. He is resplendent in a purple satin suit, a purple shirt and tie and purple patent-leather shoes. The young woman from the bar is still on his arm.

As he passes he nods in my direction. I can tell by his face he has already forgotten our profound discussion in the bar only an hour before.

'Thank you, Mr Powers.'

'Well, y're welcome,' he says, without stopping, and is ushered into a limousine outside.

Later that evening, I slip into the Lime Bar. Gustave says nothing. The ban has been lifted.

Whilst nursing a very fine gin, lime and tonic, I happen to catch a glimpse of Marty Powers on the television news.

'Turn it up!' I yell to Gustave. 'Quick!'

'. . . and just this afternoon in this very farn city of yers,' he says in his distinctive voice, 'a little lady says to me, "Mr Powers, would yer like to go to the Maldives with me? I

feel it is very important we go to the Maldives together."
And I know, my friends, I KNOW, this is part of my God-
given journey. That we must never, EVER, deny our personal
journeys . . .'

Gustave flicks the television off.

'Power to the purple,' he says before laughing, and
starts cutting some more limes with the precision of a heart
surgeon.

'Gustave,' I say, 'did you ever consider becoming a heart
surgeon?' I am being sarcastic here. I want to cut *him* somehow for making fun of Marty. Sort of. Not really. Maybe a bit.

He simply looks at me and smiles. 'But I already am,
monsieur.'

SIXTEEN

Virginie

I AM too embarrassed to tell even Gustave, let alone my psychiatrist, about my intention to live in France.

I presume it is something of an offence to withhold information from one's therapist. That it contravenes the Therapist Convention. But this. I have stunned myself. I have detonated something in the ocean of me, and risen to the surface, unconscious.

It would be easy to blame the American motivationalist Marty Powers, who stirred within me not inconsiderable dreams and ambitious notions. It is more that he drew together a picture of myself – early middle aged, almost divorced and without prospects of love – and yet promised that I, too, could embark on a personal journey. An odysseeey, as he put it.

His mere presence acted as a sort of cartoon lightbulb that has started throbbing above my head. I have to do something with my life. I have to *act*.

So it is that I find myself on a flight to Paris. I have

minimum luggage. The barest of toiletries. No itinerary. I have acted on such a whim I have not even taken into account my apparel for the flight. Usually I am fastidiously prepared. The slip-on shoes, the designer tracksuit, the small bottle of Evian spray, the inflatable peanut pillow, the tin of dusted sweets for the ascent and descent.

I am unsure if Australians are the only travellers who fly in the peculiar ensemble that is the tracksuit. Indeed it is practical, but I have often wondered how the citizens of great cities such as Paris and London and New York see us as we file through arrival lounges after a long flight. We must resemble a nation of giant babies in our baggy pants and tops.

On this occasion, however, I have dressed as if I am going to the office. (I wonder if this is part of some subconscious subterfuge.) I am perhaps the first man in the history of transcontinental flight to wear a full suit in economy class.

I am seated beside Timmy and Wendy, a young and indefatigably amorous couple from the New South Wales country town of Gulgong.

'How ya doin'?' Timmy had said the minute I sat down. 'We're from Gulgong.'

It is their first trip 'OS', as they say. 'First time in a plane,' says Wendy. I think I can detect the faint odour of cattle.

'Never been higher off the ground than the water pump back home,' Timmy continues.

They giggle and carouse and investigate everything in their seat pockets and all the buttons on their armrests. They turn the air jets above their heads on and off and find this exceedingly funny. It is going to be a long flight.

For the first leg, to Singapore, I attempt to sleep but am constantly disturbed by the activities of Timmy and Wendy. Like two children, they have covered each other with their airline blankets and are giggling and performing matters sexual beneath their coverings. I have never felt older.

'They're all like ants, hey Wendy?' Timmy had said earlier, looking out the porthole after take-off.

'Yeah, just like ants, eh?'

How true and deep and accidentally philosophical country people sometimes are in their simplicity. I begin to think I could have saved a lot of money by just driving out to Gulgong to do something substantial with my life. I could have perched on the top of Timmy's water pump and probably received as much inspiration as I needed.

Instead I have some vague notion of buying a run-down château, or some abandoned Loire farmhouse, and renovating it, and growing my own vegetables, and submerging myself in the life of my own French village, and then perhaps writing about the experience. It has been done before but not from an Australian perspective. Not from a loser-in-life-and-love Australian point of view.

As I close my eyes on the Singapore-to-Paris leg I imagine some impossibly beautiful French farm girl, in a checked-seersucker French farm girl dress, bringing handfuls of cumquats to my door, as a gesture of neighbourliness, and me inviting her in for some freshly brewed coffee in my sunlit kitchen, and her leaning back against my rustic 300-year-old stone kitchen sink, the light playing with her hair that has about it the scent of wild lemons, and me standing and walking over towards her, and her puckering her substantially swollen French farm girl lips, and me . . .

And I know then that it is not some anonymous French farm girl, but Margaret. Suddenly I am outside that kitchen, and I can see her framed in the paned window. And she is there as the window gets smaller and smaller – is it disappearing, or am I moving further away? – until it is just a pinhole of light.

I awake with a start, my nasal cavities infused with the scent of citrus. Margaret's favourite perfume. Citrus.

'One more,' Timmy is saying.

'Nuh, I'm tired,' Wendy says.

'C'mon Wend, just one more.'

'Orright.' She reaches under the airline blanket.

I have had enough of Timmy and Wendy and their matching Gulgong Roosters Rugby League Club tracksuits and indeed Timmy's incessantly roosterish behaviour. I imagine them standing atop the Eiffel Tower, hands down each other's trousers, and Timmy exclaiming, as an aside, 'Gawd, Wend, this is even taller than the water pump back home.'

I cannot get back to my dream of the sunlit kitchen and the scent of citrus. I pace the plane.

I see the vague shapes of the Austrian Alps through a rear porthole near the lavatories and a coldness runs through me. What am I doing here? What on earth can I have been thinking?

It is close to 6 a.m. when we arrive in Paris. I wish Timmy

and Wendy well, and immediately arrange a hire car. I do not want to waste any time. I will drive posthaste into the French countryside and do something with my life. I do not need sleep. Marty Powers would not sleep. Journeymen don't do sleep.

It takes me almost two hours to find the freeway to Burgundy. I remain trapped on the peripheral road around greater Paris. I go clockwise several times, take a side road off the ring, ask for directions in very bad French, return to the ring road and find myself driving anti-clockwise.

Finally, by accident, I shoot my little Citroën onto an off-ramp and discover I am at last heading south and away from the city. I feel immense elation and triumph. I feel in a minor way I have done something with my life just getting off the peripheral road. I turn up Nostalgie FM on the radio and sing along to 'Rhinestone Cowboy'.

I am about 50 kilometres short of Dijon when the snowstorm hits. Here I am, on a French highway, doing 130 kph and driving into a snowstorm. I slow down. Incredibly, the mere hint of snow seems to have electrified all the French drivers around me. They go even faster. And faster. Despite ice forming on the road. Despite the steady fall that, to my untrained eye, seems to be getting heavier and heavier.

I turn off the radio as the snowfall increases. It is a nice radio station, Nostalgie. I had been enjoying the tunes from my younger days. Funny, though, how in a vehicle with the hint of danger afoot we always turn the radio down a bit. Why is that? So we can hear ourselves scream as we slip into a culvert, then careen towards a well-established forest of pine trees?

I keep checking the dash. Only 40 kilometres to Dijon. I have to make Dijon. I am behind the wheel on the wrong side of the vehicle in a foreign car, on the wrong side of the road in a foreign car, and it is snowing and getting dark. I think this would make a good film if it was not so boring.

With 20 kilometres to go, I see a cluster of blue and red flashing lights off the highway and there is a large black BMW resting on its roof in the snow. Not much further on is another car, an Opel, on its side. And a Peugeot. I wonder what it is inside French people that clicks into hyperdrive and insanity mode whenever it starts to snow. I think of Albert Camus for some reason.

Finally I make it through into silent, snowbound Dijon and find a two-star hotel down a back lane, not far from the town's pretty central street.

The small, balding hotel owner seems to be waiting for me.

'*Bonsoir.*'

'*Bonsoir.*'

As he takes me to my room I ask him why French people drive faster in a snowstorm. I say that I have seen innumerable accidents and that surely it is quite mad that one should flirt with death so flagrantly. I ask him if all French people go fast in snowstorms, then crash as a consequence.

'Of course,' he says, as if I have asked him whether the earth actually travels around the sun.

The only redeeming feature of my hotel room is its

shower. It has the hottest water and the most powerful nozzle in France. I think of the frustrated tourists all over the country, whingeing and whining about the dribble of tepid water from their hotel bathroom nozzles, thousands of them, nude and cursing, and here I am under perhaps the most forceful jet in all of Western Europe.

It is, in fact, the nozzle that charges me with some form of personal clarity. When I am 90, I will sit back in my recliner in the nursing home and remember that chrome showerhead in the poky hotel room in Dijon as a small turning point in my life.

At the hotel owner's recommendation I scurry through the snow to a small restaurant only five doors away. Through the window I can see a fire burning in a hearth. I can hear laughter and feel the warmth of people eating together while it snows outside.

I am directed to a table. I pick up the menu. I choose the *salade* and the *coq au vin*.

'*Monsieur*?' I hear a sweet voice say.

I look up. And that's when I meet Virginie.

SEVENTEEN

The Older–Younger Man Dichotomy

AFTER three days exploring Dijon with Virginie, the wait-ress, I realise that I have entered a new sexual-attraction zone.

Somehow I have crossed its border unawares. It is as if I have been taking an overnight train journey from Milan to Munich, and have woken in the middle of the night in my cold and dark sleeper to find I have slipped silently into Switzerland.

It is the zone my father has inhabited for God knows how long. Although *he* is at the very extremity of this strange country. He has overstayed his visa, and is on the brink of deportation. While I am still a stranger here. A newcomer.

It has taken three days of walking the streets of Dijon with Virginie to fully realise I am now, officially, an older man who is attractive to certain much younger women. Why is it not a moment of celebration? Why does it rest so heavily with me as Virginie and I, hand in hand, negotiate the cobbled backstreets of the city, investigate churches and museums, stroll through the Saturday market stalls? Does it hold a bitter remnant of the Kiki La Monde experience?

I can say it literally started with the hand holding. Virginie's hand so tiny and fragile and – what? – not yet developed into a woman's. I found this disconcerting. All the strokings with the thumb and clammy squeezes that teenagers are apt to make on first discovering the erotic beauty of holding hands.

I felt conspicuous when she started swinging our held hands. I felt the entire adult population of Dijon was whispering about me from behind their counters of fine cheeses and their store-front pyramids of mustard jars. I knew no one, and yet felt I was the town molester who needed to be kept an eye on. Even the bum who operated the carousel in one of the city's many squares grimaced at the sight of us and displayed a collection of stumpy blue teeth.

Virginie remained oblivious. Perhaps this is the way with European girls? Perhaps the holding of hands in Europe does not mean what it means in Australia? Don't men hold hands in Italy? Don't girls hold hands in Hong Kong? They may hold hands, but do they swing?

My confusion moved on from the hands. Here, in this new country where older men are the object of affection of younger women, I instinctively began to over-analyse. As you do in new countries. Holding hands. With someone young enough to be your daughter.

I could see the dynamic of my father and his busty personal assistants. Here was a man on the brink of deportation, but ejected or not from the zone my father would always have, trailing behind him, a string of donkeys, their saddle-bags heavy with gold. (Why was I using such biblical metaphors? Was it the innocence of Virginie? Or the relentless religious artifacts on display in Dijon?)

I, on the other hand, did not have saddlebags as part of my allure. I am, let me say, not an unattractive man. When women are asked to comment on my looks – or so I am informed – I am one of those men who elicit the response, 'Well, he's not ugly.'

What, then, gave me entrée into this club? I am certainly greying. It is not, however, the usual grey, or so my hair-dresser, Robert, tells me. It is a distinguished 'silver' grey, he swears, as opposed to the usual muck found on the bulk of gentlemen's heads. Robert insists also that it is a silver grey that complements my bluish eyes, and vice versa. So there is the hair-eye-hair advantage at work. According to Robert.

My face, to boot, is relatively young for its age. Robert insists that it is this, the boyish face, combined with the hair-eye-hair advantage, that gives me an even further advantage. When you have the hair-eye-hair action, in tandem with the younger face phenomenon, it produces what Robert calls the older–younger man dichotomy.

'Dichotomy?' I asked one day.

'It's quite rare,' Robert said.

'I have never noticed the older–younger man dichotomy in myself.'

'Oh, but it's there,' Robert trilled. 'It is most definitely there.'

And with that he gave me a little squeeze on the shoulder.

As Robert explained it, the older–younger man dichotomy works this way: the greying hair gives off signals of maturity and experience. It is hair that says, look at me, I've been around.

'I didn't think my hair said anything,' I told Robert.

Thus, when the mature and experienced hair frames a face that does not look like it could possibly have attained the maturity and experience that the hair so loudly proclaims, the dichotomy comes into play. It says youth without the silliness. It says sprightly appeal tempered by level-headedness.

'It says I'm just getting old,' I told Robert.

'Piffle,' he said, and rolled his eyes.

'I know plenty of silly grey-haired men,' I stressed.

'But do they have the dichotomy?' Robert asked in a way that required no answer.

If Robert's dichotomy is in fact accurate, why has it not thus far made itself apparent to other people? It had proved quite fruitless back in the Lime Bar where, surrounded by younger things without an inkling of the power of my dichotomy, let alone a dichotomy of their own, I remained largely ignored on my stool. Never once had a young woman sidled up to me and congratulated me on my outstanding dichotomy.

But in Dijon I have won the attention of a waitress who is, technically, old enough to be my daughter. (I love how people say, 'She's old enough to be his daughter.' Or 'He's old enough to be her father.' Why don't they ever say, 'She's not old enough to be his mother'?)

What is it, though, that Virginie finds in me? I begin to

over-analyse once more, entering that precarious and complicated state of over-analysing over-analysis. Perhaps her father is dead, and she really does need a replacement? But then, would she tweak the bottom of her own father, or swing hands with him and stroke his palm with her thumb in this manner? No. So where does the sexual element enter this?

We have done nothing sexual, if you discount the holding of hands and the bottom tweak (her tweak, my bottom). We leaned close to a relic in the museum and I may have caught a whiff of her young woman's odour (with a trace of the restaurant kitchen, although, it being a Dijon restaurant, that was not a bad thing). And there have been several pecks on the cheek, but only in the French manner of greeting. I have also been stirred – I'll be honest – by the sheer sauciness of her accent. But that, I am sure, does not put me into the molestation category.

Perhaps I am that mysterious dynamic – the funky/crazy uncle type? The uncle who is certainly old enough to have sired such a child, but always remains like a rogue moon around the planet of the family, capable of anything. Like a teenage buffoon who, with a sense of fun and mischief, turns up for Christmas lunch with 10 kilograms of Semtex strapped to his body. Hooray, the children cry, uncle's here for a bit of fun.

(I shan't go into the relationship between funky/crazy aunts and their nephews and nieces. The funky/crazy aunt is an altogether different rogue moon, who enters interpersonal spheres that make me a touch uncomfortable.)

So what is it that has inflamed this friendship with Virginie? And where is it heading? Being totally new to the scene, I remain thoroughly bamboozled by our sudden togetherness, and remain so as we take coffee and pastries in the late afternoons. Each time, I return to my cheap hotel with the best shower nozzle in Europe, sit on the floor of the cubicle with my head on my knees and take the full brunt of the steaming jet.

Now, on this, our fourth evening together, I have escorted Virginie to a quaint little *bistrot* not far from her work. It is candlelit and an open fire burns and our red wine glows like precious stone. The glassy eyes of a deer's head stare down at us from a wall.

The *bistrot* is almost full, and I sit holding hands across the table with Virginie. I am not tired of holding hands, especially with a beautiful young French girl, but it strikes me that there has been an enormous amount of hand holding in the past few days and that, whereas in Australia young men and women secretly make love in the backs of cars or in houses momentarily empty of parents, French youth hold hands and this is their lovemaking.

Looking around, I see no one else holding hands on top of the table. I witness couples who seem to have been with each other for some time, and others who seem to have been married for an eternity, do the thing that similar couples all over the world do. They eat conscientiously, studying their plates as eagerly as they once studied the face of their partner.

I have heard so many similar conversations, in so many

different languages, between couples who have stayed with each other for too long.

'Beef's nice.'

'Mmm.'

'The coffee's cold.'

'Yes.'

'So how was your day?'

'Not bad.'

Just for once I want to see one of them rise up in the middle of such a conversation, take off their clothes, fold the items neatly in a pile, then place the pile beside the dining table, do a little backside-wiggling dance, make the wine cork disappear up a region of the human anatomy where wine corks have no place, and say to the waiter or waitress, 'I think I'll have a tub of raw vegetables and a bowl of warm chocolate sauce on the side, and thank you for asking.'

Virginie and I have plenty to say, much of which requires no words.

She eats virtually nothing. Not even a portion from the selection of fine grilled rabbit and sausages and fish that is placed between us. She looks into my face and feels my hand with her fingertips as if it were a braille book. She talks to me through my hand. My hand, at the circular caresses of her fingertips, is rendered mute.

Just when I should feel undeservedly happy (how many chances in life will I get to sit in a romantic Dijon restaurant with a young girl, not old enough to be my mother, making love to my hand?) I suffer intimations of great sorrow and regret. It is, perhaps, the lot of those cursed with the older–younger man dichotomy.

Just as the dichotomy independently does its work, there is an inner voice that dictates common sense. That says, you will pass through this zone, yet the younger women will still be younger women. You are just a tourist here. And as you leave this enchanted country, plenty more older–younger men will be waiting to come in. It is life, I reason: like the relentless waves, one after the other, that glide onto the beach. You cannot be all waves all the time. You can be nothing more than a brief sequence of waves. And then you are gone.

Afterwards we walk, Virginie and I, through the old part of the city, and then I take her home. We kiss on the cheeks and she skips up the steps to the large green wooden door of her family home.

As she opens the door she turns, waves briefly, and then disappears inside.

I stand there for some time, fixed by the image of her little wave and her disappearance, and reflect on how some moments are so outrageously pure, contain so much, that you know you will remember them even as they are happening.

I thrust my hands deep into my coat pockets and walk back to the hotel. In my dark room, staring at the ceiling, I understand that Marty Powers may be right: life may be a journey, littered with unusual events and many people and plates of grilled meats and snowstorms and shower nozzles. That if it is a journey, we are all travellers. And that I was once a very good traveller, and now am a very poor traveller. (I am thinking metaphorically. Is this good, or bad?)

I am positive I used to be a good traveller. That I could read foreign timetables as well as a local. That I peeled oranges with meticulous precision in trains in the middle of the night between, say, Zurich and Hamburg, with my Swiss Army knife. That I had never eaten salads while in India (it was only a thirty-minute stopover).

Travel is having the state of mind to actually carry your whole world with you. Having the presence to juggle that world and transport it. I think of women's hatboxes from another era when I philosophise about travel. Not steamer trunks and such things, but those lovely-shaped hatboxes that seem to be the only sort of luggage capable of carrying a whole world in.

And when you are a competent traveller it makes incompetent travellers around you even more prone to silliness and error. Accomplished travelling disconcerts them. The shinier you are, the tattier others become.

I remember once travelling through the Swiss Alps on an overnight train. I was but a youth on my first trip overseas, yet I exuded the residual orderliness of the Boy Scout.

On that evening, unable to sleep, I was sitting quietly at my window seat – my Swiss Army knife a bulge in my trousers – when the man opposite me began leafing through a magazine. He had smiled at me as I entered the compartment and that was all. He was continually busy doing something. Making notes, cleaning his spectacles, eating. Especially eating. His hand luggage, I began to realise, was in fact a mobile cafeteria.

He offered me a slice of some dark-blooded sausage,

which I declined gracefully. He returned to his magazines. We talked very little during the journey, although he told me he was a great opera fan, and that he spent his time travelling Europe, and indeed the world, to watch opera.

I wanted to know how a large man with dark sausage in his bag could afford to wander the world and take his seat in the great opera houses. There are many different people in the world, I thought wisely, on this my first trip overseas, and duly noted it in my travel diary with the koala on the front cover. A gift from my mother, naturally.

The trip was quite pleasant on this dark night, with my fellow traveller clutching his opera magazines, and the snow beside the tracks a purple hue. I had never seen so much snow. Then, suddenly and without warning, the train screeched to a halt, throwing bags from overhead racks and tipping overcoats onto the floor. The opera fan's magazines fluttered through the cabin.

I fell forward but righted myself quickly. I thought that possibly some species of wildlife had wandered onto the tracks, or that there had been an avalanche, or that a disillusioned youth who had perhaps impregnated his Swiss milkmaid girlfriend had cracked under the pressure and placed his head on the line.

In the stillness after the train stopped, I noticed my compartment companion's magazines strewn across the floor. And I noticed they were not opera magazines at all. Not journals filled with interesting tidbits about composers and acoustics, costumes and instruments. They were, in fact, naughty magazines depicting men in all manner of compromising positions. Men in the shower. Men frolicking in a barn. Men abseiling in the nude.

He hastily gathered the magazines together, stuffed them in his small bag and departed, trailing an odour of unrefrigerated sausage.

That, to my mind, was a clear case of sloppy travelling.

As a traveller I never used to waste time. I once arrived in Vienna at 7 a.m., found a pension a long way from the centre of town, checked in and left my luggage in the room, caught a bus to the heart of the city, had a look around, felt there was little else to see, went back to the pension, retrieved my bags, settled the balance, and was on a train to Berlin that evening. If I had written a tourist guide to Europe then, it would probably have been thin enough to slip into a sleeve of your wallet.

But now, in middle age, in an indifferent room in the snowbound heart of France, I realise that I have lost touch with the efficient traveller I had once been. I pack badly. I misread maps.

I fall asleep, with Virginie already a blurred face on the platform outside the window of the train that is now my life.

EIGHTEEN

A Beck's with Derain

I HAVE somehow ended up on a freeway heading south-west. I skirt Bordeaux, then continue on to Toulouse. At a petrol station outside the city I consult my driving map and its confusing ventricles of roads, and briefly consider heading across to Pau, merely because I like the sound of it. It seems, to me, a very emphatic-sounding town. A town where one could make quick and solid decisions. Pau.

I continue driving, however, having fallen in love with the motion of the vehicle, the rush of the landscape, the whole forward momentum of the journey. It is, I gradually realise, an illusion. A replacement for the movement that should be happening in my life.

From the three-lane freeway I see several distant farm-houses. Many, I am sure, would suit my purposes admirably. But I am loath to leave the freeway. The freeway, in a way, has become my safety zone. I am a middle-aged man with a French freeway for a security blanket. As a result, late in the evening I find myself steering the little sour-smelling Citroën up a steep escarpment in company with all manner of trucks and vans, and ultimately arrive at the Spanish border. This is a measure of my instability at this time. I have overshot France.

'Passport,' the border guard says.

'I'm sorry, I've come too far. Could I just . . .'

'Passport.'

'I just want to turn around, if I could, and . . .'

'Passport.'

I hand over my passport and he orders me to park the vehicle a short distance inside Spain. I wait. He approaches the car.

'Out please,' he says. I get out. He looks under the front and back seats. He unzips my small overnight bag and pokes his way through T-shirts and underwear.

'Boot, please.'

I pop the boot and he stares into its emptiness with some incredulity.

'Tourist?' he asks.

'Yes. *Si*.'

'No luggage?'

'That is luggage,' I say, pointing to the small bag.

'That is luggage?'

'That is luggage.'

'Go away,' he says, pointing towards France.

'Thank you,' I say. I have never thanked anyone for telling me to go away before.

It is now late evening and I suddenly find myself on a small road heading east, towards the coast. I don't know how I have come to stray off the freeway. I pass through a tunnel of what looks suspiciously like Australian gum trees and for a moment am completely displaced in time and space.

I am driving to Gulgong. That's what I'm doing. In a few minutes I'll be in the main street of Gulgong.

Instead, I break out of the tunnel and find myself on a ridge that looks down on the small seaside town of Collioure. I hit the brakes and sit wide eyed and breathless.

This is it, I say to myself. This is the place. This is where I am meant to be, always, for all time. I feel like Gene Kelly when he first saw Brigadoon.

I compose myself, and drive down the winding road towards my future.

And I am humming, '. . . come home to Bonnie Jean . . .'

It is very late. I check into a small hotel overlooking one of Collioure's two small half-moon bays. Then I sit on my balcony sipping a Beck's.

The palm trees rustle on the foreshore and the giant Château Royal, with its steep stone sides, juts out into the harbour. It is dusted pink by several spotlights.

I am the only Australian in Collioure sitting on a balcony in the cool night air, taking a Beck's and thinking about life. I am perhaps the only Australian doing this in all of France. I am sure there are plenty of French people sitting on balconies thinking about their lives, but not here in Collioure. Not in my village.

Less than an hour after arriving I begin to hatch outrageous and fanciful plans to live in Collioure until I am an old man, hobbling around the base of the Château Royal and joining the morning fishermen for a chat as they fold their nets for the day.

I will live in Collioure and perhaps buy a little café and call it Le Café Brigadoon, and serve thimbles of strong coffee to the locals, and become very popular, and later run for mayor. When I am mayor of Collioure I will make sure the village is preserved as Derain and Matisse painted it earlier in the century. I will use their paintings as something of a blueprint for the appearance of the town.

Then I will hire Derain and Matisse lookalikes to paint, on a shift-rotation basis, down by the edge of the beach with authentic early-twentieth-century easels. This will become a major tourist attraction. The lookalikes will speak a French marginally different from today's, with authentic inflections and word assemblages of the era.

If that is successful, I will provide employment for several of the village folk by having them dress up as regular citizens of Collioure as it was earlier in the century. They will amble up and down the seafront boulevards, a woman or two perhaps leisurely pushing a perambulator, a man walking his Irish wolfhound.

At night Le Café Brigadoon will replicate the great bohemian debates of the Derain–Matisse period. There will be heavy Gauloise smoke in the café, and lots of regional white wine and mussels and oysters, and perhaps a contraband bottle of absinthe that will be produced from behind the bar at strategic intervals.

In the middle of all this thinking about the future I tiptoe down to the foyer of the hotel and retrieve two more cans of Beck's from the beer-vending machine. How civilised France is.

Back on the balcony I feel as fresh as a minted coin and excited by my thoughts. I will, of course, marry a sophisticated Parisian woman whose attention I will have attracted as owner and maître d' of Le Café Brigadoon. She, her cheeks ruddy from the drive in her convertible from St Tropez, will have lingered for an inordinate amount of time in the café and ultimately we will have spoken.

She will have told me that she was on annual leave from her position as adviser to the Louvre, and that her maid was taking care of her apartment in the Boulevard St-Germain, and that her holiday apartment in St Tropez was lonely since she had been unattached for nearly twelve months.

I will have regaled her with tales from my past life in Australia, and she will have found me somewhat rugged and interesting, a frontiersman. We will have touched hands, then kissed, then made love, then married, and we will spend the rest of our lives driving around in her open-top car.

The next morning I decide to explore the village of which I am to become mayor, and sally around the first bay in the shadow of the Château Royal. I nod to locals catching some sun beneath the ramparts and even pat my first Collioure dog. As I round the base of the château I find the twin bay on the other side is a completely different bay in nature. It seems to be the working bay, whereas the bay that I can see from my hotel balcony is the picturesque bay.

Old fishermen display their catches on trestle tables covered with melting ice. Their merrily coloured boats bob at their moorings in the deep channel that runs alongside this shadowed side of the château.

I sit and watch the fishermen and try to make eye contact. I do not know what I will do if a conversation is actually struck. I have little command of French. Once, many years ago, I ordered ham and cheese on toast and received a bowl of sorbet. I don't think the waiter was trying to be smart.

I take a coffee in the little beachside café that has a view of the remarkable church on a tongue of rock poking into the harbour. I mouth *Bonjour* to passers-by. The waiter takes ages with my *café crème*. I will sack him the minute I buy this café and transform it into Le Café Brigadoon.

Over to my left are dozens of brightly painted yellow and blue and green townhouses facing the bay. Washing dangles from makeshift lines on the balconies: French T-shirts and French knickers and French socks. I will introduce a Non-Display of Personal Washing edict when I become mayor. I have never seen a pair of underpants in a Derain or Matisse painting.

I watch admiringly as an elderly man strips down to his trunks and begins doing laps in the icy harbour. I will follow the gentleman's lead when the time comes. I will be the old mayor who swims his laps of the harbour every morning, winter or summer, and waves to the fishermen and perhaps features in a few of the paintings of my Derain and Matisse lookalikes. *Man Swimming in Harbour, Collioure*, 1911.

I smile and think of Gustave back in Sydney and check

my watch, which is still on Australian time, and take pleasure in the thought that he will be there, in the Lime Bar, serving drunken patrons and slicing his citrus, and listening to tales of woe, and observing with a weary eye the same old machinations of courtship and love play, and that he will go home and perhaps glance at his Derain print in the hallway and I will be there, in the print, a blurred figure on the beach of Collioure.

What would he think of me now, taking coffee and watching an old man swimming back and forth across the harbour, with nothing stretching ahead of me but a peaceful and love-filled future?

I am having another coffee when it happens.

'Bugger me,' someone says. I turn around. There is nothing more rasping than an Australian accent on foreign soil. It always emerges with the subtlety of a dentist's drill striking bare nerve. I wince. A profound, bitter-lime wince.

It is Timmy and Wendy from Gulgong.

'I'll be buggered,' says Wendy.

They are both wearing Australian Rugby League jerseys, jeans and runners. They stand staring at me with mouths as wide open as those of sideshow clowns awaiting the drop of the ping-pong ball.

I can only think of one thing to say. 'Oh.'

'How ya doin', mate? Fancy seein' you here.' They pull up chairs at my table, still looking as if they have just seen the birth of a five-legged calf.

'Incredible,' says Timmy.

'Incredible,' says Wendy.

It is more than incredible. It is catastrophic. They have snapped me instantaneously out of my fantasy.

They explain that they have just come down on the train from Paris to Nice, that the train was faster than a lizard drinking, that Nice is fifty times bigger than Gulgong, that the police sirens sound funny, that the beer isn't like home's, that the food is real strange and they have both had the trots since Paris, that the postcards are real rude and they've bought twenty of them and sent them to everyone back home, that they'd really wanted to go to Cannes to see some movie stars but they'd missed the stop and just kept going 'cause it was better they saw as much as they could while they were down on the Coat Da Zoor, and that they got off at Collioure 'cause they know a bloke back home called Collier and thought they might stop and get a sambo and post him a postcard with a Collioure postmark on it 'cause that would crack everybody up back in the pub at Gulgong.

'How do you ask for a sambo in Frog?' Timmy asks.

'Dunno,' says Wendy.

'Weren't talkin' to you,' says Timmy.

We chat like this for several minutes. I have not factored the Timmys and Wendys of the world into my plans for recreating early-twentieth-century Collioure.

As the couple from Gulgong attempt to order food through the waiter – 'You got beetroot? Beeeeet-rooooooot.' – I wonder yet again whether I have really ever belonged in Australia and if, in fact, I am an Australian at all.

'If you'll excuse me,' I say, rising from my chair.

'Where ya goin'?' Timmy asks.

'I have things to do.'

'You gonna have some tucker? You've gotta have some tucker.'

'I've eaten, thank you.'

'Snails, didjya?' Timmy asks.

'Didjya?' asks Wendy.

'No,' I say. 'No snails. Nice to see you again.'

'Taste like dirt,' says Timmy.

'Yeah, like dirt.'

I almost break into a run from the café. When I reach the church – which I do not enter as Timmy and Wendy have continued to observe me from the café – I slip around the back and am hit with a blast of cool, salty ocean air.

I take the walkway around yet another scallop of beach and clamber up a small hill to where a giant crucifix faces out to sea. I look up at the iron Jesus. He has rusted around the nail wounds and has a dark orange stubble across his face.

I sit at the foot of the cross, stare out to sea and think of the communion wafers of my boyhood. I close my eyes and swear I can smell limes on the sea breeze.

Is it a loved one sending me a message from across the world? I look out to the ocean again, as all confused 13-year-old teenagers look out to the ocean, thinking with a self-conscious calf-eyed mooning of Margaret and what she might be doing, and my pals from the Governor's Pleasure, and my therapist with his white socks, and Bunger in the Australian Alps, and Marty Powers, who is probably at this moment sharing a personal destiny with

some butterfly-clipped floosy in a hotel suite in the
Maldives, and my sad masseur, Kenneth, and my father
with his Romeo y Julietas, and all the other people in my
life.

Why do we always do this whilst overseas, we Australians? Why do we try to imagine what others are doing
back home, on the flipside of the world, with flipside times
and flipside weather?

For the first time in aeons, I can also see myself back
there. Staggering from the Lime Bar with a pocketful of
coasters covered in illegible scrawl.

I slump back against the cross. And am poked, not incon-
siderably, by the stiff toe of Jesus.

I have been booted off by the rusted toe of Christ, on a
bluff above an obscure French seaside village.

I know I cannot fall any further.

NINETEEN

God and Peas

ON a postcard to Gustave I write: 'Have been kicked in the derrière by the Almighty.'

I find this rather witty under the circumstances. My psychiatrist would undoubtedly see it as a 'breakthrough'. That I am joking about existence itself. Playing with the hems of the Lord. Gustave, on the other hand, will see me as having either been touched by the faith or become 'the loser of the marbles'.

I know that the crucifix has been placed there to protect sailors and fishermen and all who venture upon the sea, yet the cold of the rusted iron has infected me, and I find myself querying my place in the eyes of God and on the earth, and indeed in the small seafood restaurant where I have decided to take a last supper, of sorts.

The proprietors are very amiable and welcome me into the restaurant as if I were related to someone in the kitchen. Either that or they suspect that I am an influential restaurant critic who sometimes writes for an international

cuisine magazine. Perhaps I have the bearing of a cosmopolitan food critic. It would explain why I am occasionally
fussed over in restaurants in Sydney. And it makes sense of
the incident outside the greengrocer, where an elderly man
insisted I inspect his leeks.

As I take a seat in the corner of the restaurant I already
feel mysterious and a force to be reckoned with. I peruse the
menu at length. I dilly-dally over it. It is written strictly in
French, so much of my time is spent attempting to decipher
the dishes. I do not let on.

By the arrival of the wine menu I am totally inside my
role as international food critic. I see, out of the corner of
my eye, the proprietor and his wife folding napkins and
shuffling about with, I presume, some anxiety. I order
swiftly by just pointing to the dishes and the wine. I have
read somewhere that silence engenders authority.

But that done, I realise it is just a game in which I am
indulging – the game of the person who eats alone in a
restaurant.

I have no book or magazine, so must resort to reading the
label on the wine after it finally arrives. I smile meekly at an
elderly couple across the room, and am ignored by a young
man and woman holding hands a few tables away. I believe I
have made the restaurant uncomfortable by staring out from
my corner.

I complete my entrée of asparagus spears with almost
indecent haste because I do not have a companion or a magazine or a book to slow my eating process. I have no one
else's plate to check to make sure I am not being piggish.

I am unable to pace my eating by discussion. The plate is removed and the main delivered almost immediately.

Having learned from the entrée, I linger over the *coq au vin*. I begin to seriously analyse my strange emotions out under the cross on the harbour.

I think, for the first time in decades, of my holy communion day, and the taste of the wafers. The sensation is so powerful they might as well be on my tongue there and then, dissolving, catching on my white small-child teeth.

Thoughts of the wafers set off a trigger-like remembrance of other aspects of my early religious life. I am reminded of Proust, and wish I had a volume of his epic work at my table. Some of my memories are not pleasant.

I remember weekly confession: sitting near the large white vinyl doors of the two confessional booths, waiting my turn. They were studded in the way a couch is, and had plastic purple doorknobs shaped like faceted diamonds.

Once inside, I always confessed to the same things, week after week, year after year. That I misbehaved in class, and did not eat my peas at home.

I would always get the same penance for my crimes. One decade of the rosary. Funnily, I always associate peas with confessions to God. Now I count peas like rosary beads, whenever they find their way to my table. Odd the things that stay with you.

There was a moment, as a boy, when I even contemplated being a priest. The contemplation did not last long, and probably carried as much weight as a similar desire to be a veterinary surgeon. Every pet I ever owned died, either through misadventure or my own reckless disregard. I was not about to take the same risk by joining the priesthood.

Still, I wore a small silver cross around my neck for some years and tucked it, day after day, beneath my white Bond's singlet. I felt, somehow, it was important to wear the cross and that it would assist with my early loathing for peas. Since I eventually came to adore peas, it must have been successful.

Then, at a certain point, religion faded out of my life. All that tradition, all that ritual, all that godliness that came from dropping coins into collection plates and dipping one's finger in holy water just vanished.

I had not thought about religion again until my moment under the cross, here in Collioure. When I sat at the feet of Jesus bleeding with rust. It has to mean something.

Gustave would be delighted to know that I am thinking about the absence of religion, having sat at the feet of Jesus. Confirmed Catholic that he is, he would say that God is calling me back to the fold. Typical Frenchman. And Catholic.

What, then, would I say to him?

'You are deluded, Gustave.'

'*Non, non,*' he would say. 'This is the Lord calling you back where you belong.'

'How can I come back? I haven't been to confession for thirty years.'

'God does not count.'

'God knows everything, doesn't he? He must be able to count.'

'He may know how to count. But he does not count.'

'Does he know how many years, days, minutes and sec-onds I am going to live?' I would ask.

'Of course. He is God.'

'Then God counts,' I would say triumphantly.

I realise I have finished the *coq au vin* and the plate has already been taken away. If I had been reading a Bible at the table would I have been given a free dessert?

I also realise, on hitting the sea air outside the restau-rant, that I have consumed far too much wine. I notice the proprietor and his wife watching me anxiously through the restaurant window as I steady myself against one of the waterfront palms. I know what they are thinking. That I am no international food critic. Not even a wine critic. I am a tourist who has sat at the foot of the cross out on the harbour and had thoughts about his religious past and peas in the confessional and now feels he has perhaps wasted his life and is travelling the world searching for meaning and finding it only in wine bottles; is spending his life staggering out of restaurants looking for palm trees to right himself against.

I feel an overwhelming need to speak to Gustave. It would be morning back home. He would be at the Lime Bar, preparing for the day's trade. I can smell the sharp tang of the lime juice.

'Gustave, it's me!' I say when he answers the phone. 'I'm coming home!'

'Have you been away?' he says.

TWENTY

Natural History of the Not Quite Dead

IF I were to tell anyone that I see myself as an old man, in the bright toilet cubicle of an aircraft 10 000 metres over India, they would not believe me.

I had slipped quietly out of France. (I like saying 'I had slipped quietly out of', even though nobody would have noticed my absence.)

Many hours into the journey I slipped quietly into the aircraft lavatory. I made sure I did this well in advance of mealtime. For it is the habit of travellers to stampede the lavatories immediately after taking a meal. It is impossible to relieve one's self for at least an hour after dining on an aircraft. I got in early, and I wish I hadn't.

For here, in the mirror, is a haggard, depleted man with nothing but a stupendous blankness to his face. If faces are blackboards, this one is clean, save for the ghostly chalk swipes of a recent wiping.

I am not overly concerned at the dullard who stares back at me. No, that is not it. It is the small, previously undetected scar line below my right ear that attracts my attention. What is it? I examine it more closely. Have I been inflicted with an injury without noticing? I turn my head hard to the left to trace the scar. Is it? No. Is it a stretch mark?

There is a light tap on the lavatory door. I ignore it.

Turning my head hard right, I notice I have an almost identical line below my left ear. When did this occur? How were stretch marks on your neck allowed to happen without your being informed? When had my head put on weight, pulled the skin tight, and then lost weight enough to produce stretch marks? I did not know heads put on weight.

I stare directly into the mirror. Suddenly I can see other blemishes and lines and nicks and scratches. I am like a satellite camera plummeting towards earth, unstoppable, perfectly focused, capturing the world, then a continent, then a state, a mountain, a boulder, the surface of the boulder, the grains of quartz in the boulder. Then boom. Nothing.

There are spectacular fans of lines spreading outwards over my temples from the corners of my eyes. Deep ruts of age, frilled with finer gullies. A crooked wrinkle has emerged between my eyes. It is odd, wavering, as if its loyalties are torn between one eye and the other.

And my lips. I observe, for the first time, several micro-thin crevices that fissure up and down from the lip line. I have become, overnight, a crosshatched newspaper caricature.

'Hello?' a feeble voice queries on the other side of the lavatory door.

'A minute,' I shout.

How can this be? How can I leave Australia for France a

relatively well-manicured male and return, after a mere fort-night, a premature old man?

'Hello,' says the voice again.

'Just a second!'

It is, I decide, absolute proof of my theory of ageing. I have always believed we don't age day by day, minute by minute. I think we can go for years without any discernible ageing and then, in the space of forty-eight hours, perhaps a week at the most, we have a cell breakdown, a colossal col-lapse, a physiological earthquake, that ages us years in a matter of hours. I call it the elastic-band effect. We stretch and snap, stretch and snap. Then the process starts all over again. Until one day the elastic band breaks for good.

It is, at least, a better explanation than my head having gained and lost weight.

It is a theory I have used many times to kill a dinner party. It works unfailingly. It sends men and women alike scurrying to bathroom mirrors.

And here I am, before the mirror myself, witnessing the outfall of my latest elastic-band stretch and snap, which must have happened en route to the airport in Paris, perhaps in the back of the taxi, for I remember little about the ride beyond fleeting images of Margaret and the state of my flat back in Sydney. And a few *clochards* scrounging through rub-bish bins near the beautiful, bat-like art-deco arch of a Metro station. And two girls walking along the street swinging their held hands.

'Excuse me!' says the voice on the other side of the door.

'All right!'

I fling the door open and confront an elderly lady, no taller than my shoulder, with a face like a badly crazed dinner plate. I am unsympathetic. I have my own elastic-band snaps to deal with.

I return to my seat and refuse dinner. I have no appetite. I am now a man with stretch marks on his neck and a wiggly line between his eyeballs.

I close my eyes and contemplate decay.

Haven't there been signs? Oh yes, indeed. There have been signs all right. The recurring agony in the joint of my left toe. There is that, certainly. And the impending arthritis in the right thumb. Too stiff to move sometimes. Too locked up to give attractive women shoulder massages after a fine meal and the offer of coffee in my apartment. (Which, by the way, I have never done. But it's funny how my flat becomes an apartment only when I imagine asking women in for coffee.)

And what of the knees? The knees that click like summer garden insects every time I get up from a seated position. Knees that crack and pop and turn people's heads because they sound like a closing door, or a small gunshot from a lady's pearl-handled purse pistol.

'You sure you won't have anything to eat, sir?' the flight attendant asks again.

'No, thank you,' I say, like some man minutes from the electric chair.

Stairs are harder to climb. Stairs are to be avoided at all cost. I have even run for a taxi in the city, then heaved for ten minutes in the back seat, fearing a stroke. It makes no scientific sense that one can run for thirty seconds and gasp for ten minutes. If this was commensurately correct, marathon runners would run for two and a half hours and catch their breath for several years.

'You must get yourself into the semblance of the shape,' Gustave has said to me so often.

Like he could talk. Like any Frenchman could talk. They smoke on Nautilus machines. Blow smoke rings atop horses when riding through the Bois de Bologne. Sneak a couple of puffs crossing the English Channel. Swimming, that is, not on the ferry or through the chunnel.

'Into shape? What for?'

'At the beginning of the life you get into the shape because you're the young buck, stronger than the other bucks, trying to attract the female.'

'How interesting,' I reply.

'But then you have to get into the shape to chase off death.'

'Thank you so much, Gustave. You certainly know how to cheer up an evening.'

But here, in my economy seat in the plane over India, thinking of mortality, I know he is right.

I begin to panic. Should I start now? Should I commence pacing around the plane, doing sit-ups in the aisle or performing those weird, Asian-inspired morning exercises that you see people doing in public parks at obscene hours? Those odd martial-arts-style slow kicks and arm extensions that I have always sniggered at on my way to the office with my give-me-a-break facial expression?

I look around the plane. It is full. I will be very conspicuous if I begin now.

This is ridiculous. Why is it that people would rather die than be embarrassed in front of other people? I should start now. I have to do something. I'm dying, I want to shout – can't you see I'm dying?

I stay in my seat. Settle down. Be rational. Get your once-fat-now-thin-again head together. You are not going to die at this instant. In fact, you have less chance of dying right now than your fellow passengers who have tucked into the beef curry and the roast chicken airline dinners. As for the plane crashing, don't they always say that you have a greater chance of dying in a road accident than in a plane crash? (Well, why wouldn't they say that? How many planes pass each other in the opposite direction at a distance of a couple of metres in the course of one flight? How many red lights do planes run? There, I am getting worked up and being hysterical again.)

I will do nothing. I will remain seated and feel sorry for myself. I am getting old. Who does not get old? I have seen babies in prams who looked not a day under fifty. I should be grateful that I am not one of those old-man babies. They give me the creeps, old-man babies. Compared to old-man babies, I have been pretty lucky. I realise I should have eaten. I am feeling delirious.

On the run from Singapore to Sydney I take a couple of Jack Daniels on the rocks, snap out of my melancholy and decide to face my life in the manner that the astute businessman that I am would face a problem. Okay, this is what to do. No more attending the Lime Bar and drinking myself into a stupor. The Lime Bar is out.

On landing, buy an entire new set of tennis, squash, cycling and possibly martial-arts apparel. Shoes right through to shorts and T-shirts and windcheaters. Start watching the ABC and going to bed at 9.30 p.m. Get up just before dawn and drink fresh juice made from real fruit in a real fruit juicer. Start eating more cereals.

Okay. No more long lunches that spill into dinner. No more coffees. Meet a nice, old-fashioned Margaretesque woman who likes to go ballroom dancing on the weekends, takes long bush walks and bakes her own bread.

Okay, okay. Join library and chamber music committees and lower the personal tension. Sit and watch sunsets. Go in fun runs. For fun. Get involved in life. Get involved.

By the time the plane lands I am exhausted by all the things I have to do. I trudge wearily through Customs and out into the arrivals hall.

And there he is, suddenly, glowing like a polished martini glass.

'Welcome home!' says Gustave as I fall, slowly, into his friendly, but not overly friendly, French embrace.

He realises with alarm he is holding up my entire body weight, and for a moment we dance oddly, like two entangled puppets with their strings cut, around the arrivals hall.

'A long trip,' he says.

TWENTY-ONE

The Follicles of Men

GUSTAVE, my barman, is unhappy.

I have rarely seen Gustave unhappy. Once, a year ago, he sulked when, during one of his splendid Sunday lunches, his duck *confit* did not turn out as expected.

There was, too, a brief flash of anger when, as a backgammon novice, I defeated him, using his very special handcrafted ivory and leather set. He had foolishly opened a rare bottle of red before the match in anticipation of victory, and the dregs of it sat heavily in his glass in the bitter glow of his misery.

But Gustave is upset this time because I have rejected his invitation to a gala French-themed New Year's Eve party at his home for this, the dawn of a new millennium.

I had, admittedly, initially accepted the invitation and had even arranged a costume. I would go as Joan of Arc. I figured it was appropriate not only to my past year, but the whole nineties in my life.

It was conceivable there would be dozens of Joan of Arcs

at Gustave's party. The French love nothing more than dressing up as Joan of Arc.

I visited a Joan of Arc web site for research and have struck up a rather unusual correspondence with a woman who thinks that Joan of Arc speaks to her. (But that's another story I would prefer not to get into.) Considering Joan of Arc also claimed to have heard divine instruction, I am not overly worried about this. I myself am more attracted to the burning-at-the-stake end of Joan's life. 'The arc of her life,' I said to Gustave, which, I now remember, was the third time he ever became unhappy with me.

Then another invitation came my way, one which perfectly dovetailed with my recent resolution on the flight back from France to make the 2000s a happy 2000s for myself. No more 1900s disasters.

I only started seriously considering how I would define myself, indeed 'streamline my being' (my psychiatrist's new buzz phrase) in the 2000s, during a recent acquisition made over the telephone using my credit card. When the young merchant on the other end of the line asked me for the expiry date of the card I duly quoted it – November 2000. I could hear her writing down the details. She was one of those people who mumble exactly what they are writing during the very act of writing. I distinctly heard her say, 'November, oooh, oooh.' It was this, the 'oooh, oooh', that inexplicably unlocked a small door of hilarity within me, and I felt my depression lift instantly. I thanked her and asked her if I could quote her 'oooh, oooh'.

'Of course. I'd be honoured,' she said.

'Let me practise,' I said.

'Go ahead.'

'My birthday next year is the fifth of the seventh, oooh, oooh.'

'That's very good. I think you've got the swing of it.'

'This bottle of tomato sauce has an expiry date of the eleventh of the eleventh, oooh, oooh.'

'That's the way,' she said.

'You've made my millennium,' I told her.

'You're very welcome.'

There are, I have decided, still some nice people in the world.

As for Gustave. Poor Gustave. I agreed to attend his French-themed party in lieu of nothing else turning up, and then received a beautifully printed, gold-trimmed invitation to a full-black-tie soirée aboard a giant catamaran on Sydney Harbour. More than 200 guests. Jazz and rock bands. Fine Australian champagnes. And a pass to one of René Rivkin's city nightclubs after the cruise. I would be going as the guest of my therapist, on a boat listing with therapists.

It's not that I thought it was a swankier occasion than dinner at Gustave's, or that I would meet more interesting and attractive women or have a better view of the fireworks. From Gustave's rear balcony there is the glimpse of a harbour view to be had, although I had a mental image of dozens of Joan of Arcs straining to see the pyrotechnics and shuddering with each fiery bloom.

No. The fact of the matter is I figured that if I could not

muster the strength to wage my physical and mental battle against decay on a cheery, bobbing boat with 200 therapists on board, if I could not gather in their company the chutz-pah to turn around that man I had seen in the toilet cubicle on the flight back from France, then I was never going to be able to change my life.

I have pleaded with Gustave for understanding but he has yet to come around.

He has refused to serve me my customary gin, lime and tonics. He is suddenly occupied when I require a top up. Instead, he leaves it to his apprentice, Jules, to keep me watered. Jules is a nice kid. But a barkeep who doesn't know the difference between vodka and gin is going to find it tough out there.

In keeping, though, with my new positiveness, I push Gustave's disappointment from my mind and begin making preparations for the big night. Indeed, I envisage it as a sort of tuxedoed rebirth. Indeed I see myself, in the New Year, as brighter than a Ken Done tea towel. (I also privately vow, as a resolution of sorts, to remove the word 'indeed' from my lexicon.)

My first move is to change my entire appearance. I cannot immediately alter the thickening midriff but I can do some-thing about my hair. I visit Sean, my new hairdresser (surely new hairdressers can give new looks?), who suggests quite whimsically, as one would suggest a picnic in the park, that I get my hair 'straightened'.

'Straightened?'

'Yes,' Sean says. 'To remove that kink.'

'Kink? I have a kink?' I feel quite panicked. My scalp prickles.

'Yes. This *delightful* little kink you have.'

He is obviously unaware of my sensitivity about my 'kink'. Of course I know about the kink. When you have a kink you know about it. Hair kinks are not shy, retiring things. They are the first to the piano at a party. Whilst my kink is not exactly Liberace, it does have a little of the show-offy Shirley MacLaine about it.

I have possessed the kink since childhood and it has been a source of deep and internal suffering throughout much of my life. (I had two extremely kink-partial grandparents on my mother's side and imagine this was the source of my genetic hair disposition.) Nevertheless, I had decided to ignore its existence. To make it invisible by pretending it was not there.

I consider my new hairdresser's suggestion for some moments.

'Can it be done?'

'Take about an hour.'

'You can de-kink my hair? In an hour?'

'In an hour.'

'Straight hair? One hour?'

'Straight.'

'Just like normal straight hair? The same as other normal straight-haired people have?'

'The very same.'

I am genuinely incredulous that I would feel the wind moving my de-kinked locks by mid-afternoon.

'Shall we?' Sean says, sensing my nervous excitement.

'We shall,' I say, trying out my new derring-do 2000s self.

Sean produces a large tub of white goo and a spatula and proceeds to paste a sort of full-head bathing cap over my skull. It feels very thick and sticky and somewhat heavy. After ten minutes it also feels as if someone has poured a beaker of acid over my cranium.

My eyes start to water profusely.

'Getting to you yet?'

'Whatever it is, yes, it is getting to me.'

'Only another ten minutes. It'll sting for a bit, but that's the price you pay.'

'Are you sure this is going to work?'

'This stuff is American. It was produced specifically for African-Americans. It has been used by Oprah Winfrey.'

'If that's the case we may as well do my chest as well.'

'Really?' Sean possibly, or possibly not, licks his lips at this proposition. I cannot be sure.

'I'm joking.'

What my new hairdresser fails to tell me is that I will be forced to sit in the salon for agonising minutes with white goo pasted across my entire head while women around me get their respective haircuts, trims, streaks and perms. I figure this is the very final stretch of hair embarrassment that I will ever have to suffer.

'We nearly done?' I eventually whisper to Sean, and he duly wheels me to the sinks, where the acid is removed.

'You won't know yourself,' he says.

I do not have the heart to tell him I already do not know myself to a vast degree.

'Is it really that effective?' I ask.

'The best. I had a guy in here recently who had worse hair than yours, oooh, infinitely worse . . .'

'Oh.'

'. . . and he couldn't believe the results. He sat at the mirror staring at himself for ages. It was remarkable. He almost, well, he almost cried right there in the chair.'

I wonder if Oprah ever cries in the salon.

As Sean rinses me into my new future I have further delightful thoughts of rebirth. Not just the hair, but my entire wardrobe. I will throw out all my clothes and refit myself. I imagine how I will look in one of those smart German suits worn in magazine advertisements by all those straight-haired German models. I will wear straight-legged trousers and black patent-leather shoes with straight toes. I will go completely straight.

'Heeeeeerrre we go,' says my new hairdresser in the manner of all hairdressers. Then, with the untowelling, there comes a more than audible gasp from behind the sink.

'Is everything okay?' I ask.

No answer.

'Sean? Am I straight?'

Without speaking he wheels me very slowly back in front of the mirror, and we both stare at my hair with Munch-like faces. My hair is most definitely straight. But it is also most definitely green.

'Sean, I have green hair.'

'Yes.'

'Sean.'

'Yes?'

'Tell me my hair is not green.'

'Ooooh.'

'Sean, Sean.'

'I . . .'

'Sean.'

'This has never happened before. I . . .'

He explains that the powerful chemical must have reacted with my grey hair. He has never straightened *grey* kink hair before.

'Some coffee?' he asks timidly.

'Tea, please.'

'English Breakfast?'

'Green, thank you.'

I have at least not lost my sense of humour.

TWENTY-TWO

Eve of the Eve

I HAVE never had a good New Year's Eve.

Considering we only get about seventy or eighty of them in our lives – if we're lucky – this is not surprising. If you discount, say, the first fifteen, when very little happens on New Year's Eve, that only leaves fifty-five to sixty-five in the strike rate.

If you then subtract the last fifteen, when by rights infirmity should take the gloss off the evening, you are down to forty or fifty. If you were a bookmaker, you would have to conclude that the odds of an excellent New Year's Eve in your lifetime are quite slim.

I'm sure bookmakers have excellent New Year's Eves. These are people who understand the odds.

I have tried every combination of New Year's Eve in the quest for a singular defining experience. There is the Go to Fifteen Parties in One Night sequence. This is a delicate balance of timing and personalities, of alcohol supply and adequate transport. It has never worked.

I have tried the Throw Your Own Party experience. This, invariably, is a scatty affair, populated as it is by itinerants – people who are coincidentally practising the Go to Fifteen Parties in One Night sequence, and yours happens to fall in the middle.

There is the I'm Going to Turn My Back on New Year's Eve and Spend It With a Loved One Alone on a Deserted Beach sequence. This is potentially catastrophic. You end up sitting in the sand with a warming bottle of champagne and plastic cups, staring at a dark horizon, having run out of things to say. Watching a single flare rise off the deck of a distant prawn trawler is hardly a defining moment. The problem here is also stroke-of-midnight anxiety. As the seconds tick down you may experience an overwhelming rush of depression. That everything is really happening 'somewhere else', and you are missing out.

There is the I'll See What Happens option. This is usually the most literal option. Nothing usually happens.

There is the I'll Just Have a Few Friends Over for a Quiet One sequence. This can end in tears. You wind up sitting around a dining table, or on fold-out chairs in the backyard, looking over the people who are present and thinking, do I really want to see in the New Year with this lot? Are these really the sort of people I surround myself with in this precious thing we know as life?

Finally, there is the I'll Do It in Style and Wear a Suit/Cocktail Dress alternative. This is the one I take to usher in the new millennium. This is the choice that will change my life.

I have, of course, in my excitement, completely over-looked the logistics of the evening. How can I get from my flat in East Balmain to the wharf in Rose Bay where I am to join the ocean-going catamaran and more than 200 guests, most of them therapists? My suburb has been closed down to non-residents since midday for the celebration, and there are no taxis operating in the inner city.

This difficulty only occurs to me as I am pressing my white dinner shirt. There are further obstacles to overcome before this problem can be solved. As is always the case with myself and clothes prior to an important occasion, some-thing inexplicable happens to the winged collar of my shirt. The iron decides to disgorge a streak of iron gunk across the front of the collar.

No, this is not new to me. I have hastily thrown jumpers and skivvies into driers at the last minute and had them emerge as doll's clothes. I have dislodged buttons with taxis tooting for me out in the street.

But the iron gunk. I hastily pour soda water across the offending stain. It seems better. I iron over the damp collar. The gunk has been reduced, but the shirt turns a pale yellow where the iron strikes the soda water on the collar.

I proceed. I figure that it will be dark out on the ocean-going catamaran and that nobody will notice. I don't know how I am going to get there, but at least no one will notice my shirt.

Next I attempt to style my new straightened hair. After it turned green at the hands of my new ex-hairdresser, he put what he called a neutral rinse through it, to remove the green. It certainly achieved that. It also turned my hair such a rich mahogany that I look like I am wearing a rather close-fitting furred cap. In the wilds of Alaska. Where I am hunting bear. In the nineteenth century. There is no time to rectify it.

Now, with my black suit laid out on the bed, I take a friend's advice about the hair and wash it twenty-three times with shampoo.

'That'll tone it down,' she had said.

'It'll also leave me with no scalp.'

The shampooing does not seem to tone my hair down, but I am running out of time. I mousse it back, slip on my still-damp, yellow-collared shirt, and head out into the night, hoping to snare a rogue taxi.

There are people already unconscious in Gladstone Park. I am the only one in Darling Street wearing a tuxedo. I know everyone is staring at my mahogany hair and stained shirt. I have to get to the wharf in one hour or they will sail without me.

I just keep walking, envisaging a lonely evening on the shores of Rose Bay, sharing some port with a few old fishermen, for there are always fishermen on the harbour no matter what night of the year. I will try to walk back home afterwards, and be attacked in Rushcutters Bay Park. I will be stripped of suit and shoes and have to cross the Anzac Bridge in my undershorts.

Then I wonder how many people in the city will be doing just that anyway in twelve hours – wandering through the city in their undershorts.

As I get closer to Victoria Road, with no cab in sight, I wonder if I could hitchhike, having never hitchhiked before. I pass the Lime Bar. It is already packed. I know Gustave must be home by now, hanging his French streamers around the house, his famous *coq au vin* simmering on the stove. I feel immensely saddened.

Then, from nowhere, someone calls my name. I turn. It is Gustave.

'My poor little friend,' he says.

'Gustave! Happy New Year.'

'You have an egg yolk on your collar.'

'It's a long story.'

'It is from the dirty iron of a bachelor, I can tell these things.'

'You're right again, Gustave. You're always right.'

'You are off to your fancy harbour cruise?'

'If I ever get there.'

He waves me over to the window of his black Peugeot 504.

'We have been friends a long time, no? And it is a new century tomorrow.'

'It is.'

'Hop in, *mon ami*, I will take you to your boat.'

'But you must have a million things to do . . .'

'The *coq au vin* is being looked after. The duck is on its way. Hop in.'

Tears fill my eyes as I enter the cabin of his Peugeot and the familiar cloud of his aftershave. He is a wonderful friend and mixes the best gins in Sydney. In the history of the lime, which is yet to be written, he will feature prominently.

'You have no idea what this means to me,' I say.

'It means you will make your little soirée on the boat.'

'It wouldn't have been possible without you.'

'Sometimes *you* are not possible without me.'

I ponder this at some length. There is some merit to it.

'I'm sure your party will be wonderful, too,' I say.

'Of course.'

'You have the best parties, Gustave.'

'Obviously nothing that can match a gathering of 200 therapists on a boat.'

'Yours will be better.'

'If your head is not straight by the end of the evening, I would say there is something gravely wrong with you.'

'Think of it. A month's counselling for free. In one night. With champagne and cigars to boot.'

'It should be fun. Or will it be a nightmare? What will the therapists be saying to each other? Is this fun? Are we having fun yet? What is the nature of fun? Are we in a psychological state to have fun? What is the meaning of fun? And then, poof! The night is over.'

Gustave is right. Perhaps the entire evening will turn out to be nothing more than a floating therapists' convention. Perhaps they will all be taking notes, unable to break the habit of a lifetime of taking notes.

Or maybe the therapists will have invited some of their patients, just as I have been invited by my psychiatrist. Perhaps the therapists are conducting one giant proactive experiment on board the catamaran under the guise of a New Year's Eve party.

Gustave senses my disquiet.

'You worry too much,' he laughs. 'Let your hair down. By the way, your hair is letting itself down in a most unusual fashion these days. May I ask what has happened to it?'

'It's another long story.'

'You are full of long stories, my friend. My motto? Fill your life with short stories. The more the better.'

'Fill my life with short stories?'

'Yes. Even vignettes. A string of vignettes makes the best life.'

Who needs a psychiatrist when he has Gustave?

'Have a delicious vignette tonight,' he says. 'Promise me.'

'I promise.'

'And no one will notice your shirt. It will be getting dark after eight.'

'Thank you, Gustave.'

'Here, here is your little boat.'

He stops the car at the wharf and gives me his customary two-cheek kiss.

'Bon voyage, *mon ami*.'

'See you in the new century.'

'Yes. In the new century.'

And he is gone. I have made the cruise by fifteen minutes. Groups of beautifully attired people are milling on the dock and on board the glittering catamaran.

I cannot see my therapist on the dock. You've seen one

therapist, you've seen them all. I start looking at the men's shoes. I will be able to identify my psychiatrist because he will, as always, be wearing his white tennis socks.

I step on board and take a glass of champagne. It is a fine night. The entire city seems to be on the streets or out on the water. I am breathing in the salty harbour air when a hand takes hold of my right elbow.

'Good evening,' a low voice says.

'Oh, hello.'

'I'm Eve.'

'Eve. A pleasure.'

We stand looking into each other's eyes. There is no need for words. We do not move from where we stand. A whistle sounds, and the boat eases out into the harbour.

'Eve,' I say.

And she smiles as we sail softly into the Year 2000.

TWENTY-THREE

Man Underboard

I HAVE always been a devotee of tales of shipboard romance.

It may have started with my father's youthful stories of frolics on board ships bound for London. In the days when ships were still a viable passage for Australians to the outside world, my father would regularly join his young ladyfriends bound for Europe, on the Sydney-to-Perth leg, and then travel home by train across the Nullarbor.

In those days of illicit booze and sexual encounters, I imagine my father saw very little of the top deck.

When he cavorts with his young personal assistants, I see him back there in the bowels of the ships of his younger days, feeling up skirts and unclipping brassieres in the dark in those secure and safe little cabins all wrapped in riveted steel. Back on board a love boat at the end of his life. A love boat with faulty compasses and an irrational rudder.

But my attraction is to more than the romance. It is the microcosmic world of the cruise ship that is alluring: the country town afloat with its own constabulary and corner store, its sporting arena and nightclub, its library and suburbs.

My father packed me off on a cruise when I was a teenager. He perhaps assumed this was a natural sequel to our rather basic sex talk on the golf course. It was a peculiar though ultimately instructive gesture.

For two weeks I sailed with several hundred other souls around the Fijian islands. In that fortnight of compressed time, I was introduced to alcohol and smoking and women. I arrived on board, a neatly pressed schoolboy with model aeroplane glue under my fingernails, and staggered down the gangplank at the end of the trip with plans to open a bar with two of my new shipboard mates, to begin a cigar vending machine business, to study the finer points of poker, to leave home, to drink only sour mash bourbon, with ice made from distilled mountain water, to start using Brylcreem and to keep a detailed journal of the sexual conquests that I knew awaited me post-cruise.

None of the above transpired.

Oh, the ship had its perils, though. I recall how hypnotising I found the churned ocean water of the ship's wake; how it seemed to dare you to jump over the polished wooden rail. Which is precisely what one young man did several days out from home port. He had, in an alleged drunken stupor, decided to hop up onto the rail in the early morning hours. Then, to the shock of his companions, he simply dived into the darkness.

The story spread quickly throughout the ship, but regrettably, as the captain informed the young man's grieving friends, it would take more than half a day to physically turn the ship around. There were handfuls of hibiscus tossed into the Pacific in his memory. Yet despite the pall of his death that hung over the cruise, ship life continued apace, perhaps in tribute to him. I think of the missing boy still, after so many years, his hand raised, hopeful of rescue.

It is why I refuse to see the film *Titanic* again. I was fine for the first couple of hours, wishing I could be young Jack, floating through life, sketching nude women on couches and steaming up the glass of vintage cars.

How I loved all the pomp, the silver cutlery and fine white china, the brandies and bow ties. I did not even mind the iceberg striking and the chaos afterwards, although the moment when the ship was upended and some anonymous man lost his grip and fell dramatically, striking his head on the monstrous propeller and spinning to his demise, has stayed with me.

It was Jack's chilly death that ruined it for me, and probably for millions of men addicted to shipboard romances all over the world. His silent freezing over and disappearance into the murky depths took me back to the cruise of my youth and that unknown boy's swan dive into the Pacific. Perhaps he was the lucky one. Forever young, no longer pining for those two weeks aboard ship when life condenses itself and there is no past and future. Only present love, or the promise of it, beneath the timber deck boards.

On this warm New Year's Eve when I meet Eve, my youthfulness flickers again and my past is obliterated. No more troubling memories of my soon-to-be-ex-wife, Margaret; my quest for love in a world that no longer wants divorce-impending middle-aged men; my failed therapy sessions and attempts to reconcile my differences with my father; my decimated squash game.

No more using the word 'indeed', and pondering the future and how there must be someone out there for me, although that someone is probably on the other side of the world right now, perhaps eating her mama's *osso buco* in a peasant house in some remote village somewhere, or in Glasgow cross-stitching a princess in a castle, or sleeping on a pillow stuffed with Swedish goose feathers.

It is Eve who takes my hand and, with that single touch, delivers me afresh, into an evening of stars and fireworks.

We say virtually nothing to each other for a long time after meeting. We go quietly downstairs and sit in the boat's plush saloon, oblivious to the hordes of other revellers. Even thoughts of Gustave, my barman, are not intrusive.

I look into Eve's face and she into mine. I have no idea of her past. No idea how old she is or what her place in life is. As the boat moves quietly around the inner fringes of Sydney Harbour, in and out of bays, past the homes of millionaires, wharfside restaurants, national parks, dark beaches and blocks of flats, I simply breathe in and out in the aura of Eve. I am content to do nothing, to say nothing. I feel at peace for the first time in years.

When we do speak, it hardly measures as a dialogue. It is simply to return ourselves momentarily to some jetty of reality. To tether ourselves.

'I guess it's close to midnight,' I say.

'I guess,' she says.

'It's not raining.'

'No, it's not.'

'The harbour is beautiful.'

'Beautiful.'

'The champagne is very fine.'

'Very fine.'

'This feels quite strange.'

'Quite strange.'

Earlier, if I had not been so enamoured with Eve, so oblivious to everything, I could on two occasions have stood on the deck and seen, in the distance and with binoculars, the back of Gustave's house and his little balcony, laden with several young women dressed as Joan of Arc. But I am not of the planet.

'There will be fireworks. Soon,' I say.

'Oh yes, the fireworks.'

'We could go up and see them. If you like.'

'If you like.'

'Fireworks.'

'Yes, fireworks.'

We both would benefit from instruction from a speech therapist. Such are the follies of attraction.

We do not move from the saloon. We remain facing each other, holding hands and occasionally touching knees, simply taking each other in.

I wonder what instantly attracts two people? I have recently read much about it, about individual odours and other matters. I am unsure about the importance of odours.

There is certainly little, if any, displaying of plumage between Eve and me (if you discount my hair, as rich as an antique jarrah bureau). No strutting and rutting and pretty birdsong. We have come together as if we have known each other our entire lives.

She is one of those people I feel instantly at ease with, as if her presence is a strange sedative. She seems to feel the same about me, although I have never considered myself a sedative type. (Gustave, no doubt, would have other ideas on the subject.)

So how to explain it? Here we are, two lovers aboard ship, having done nothing more than touch hands. Here we are with what feels like years of a shared past, and only a few hours of history between us.

I suddenly notice that the entire below deck has become deserted – even the staff have disappeared – and then a tumultuous string of explosions erupts from somewhere across the water.

'We made it,' I say, somewhat cryptically.

'Yes, we did.'

'I can't believe I've met you.'

'I can't believe it either.'

We are both illuminated by the brilliant fireworks over the harbour – two children in the half-dark, touching knees.

There is shouting, and cries and music and mayhem, and it all forms a chaotic symphony that is not unpleasant to the ear and seems to make complete sense at this moment.

As the smell of gunpowder drifts into the saloon, our lips meet for the first time.

I have no idea what lies ahead for Eve and me. The boat sails back to the wharf at Rose Bay after the fireworks display. We return to the upper deck, our hands still locked, and the memory of the kiss is strong; already a part of a shared history, already sketched and framed and placed above the fireplace.

Before the boat docks, I turn to look back at the Harbour Bridge and for the first time all evening make sense of my surroundings.

There is the blazing sign that has been seen, presumably, all over the world: Eternity. And yet something has gone wrong. Something is out of place. I look at the word – it has somehow malfunctioned and only half of it remains illuminated. Nity.

Nity. Nity. I lead Eve off the boat and back to solid ground. I feel unsteady on my feet.

And for the first time all evening harsh reality intrudes. Something bothers me. An unscratchable itch has emerged.

Nity.

TWENTY-FOUR

Martinis in a Rowboat

'YOU really want to do this?'

'Yes,' I say to Gustave.

'As you wish,' he says.

And so it is that we cast off from Darling Street wharf in a small wooden rowboat on the first day of the new millennium.

How Gustave procured a small wooden rowboat with thirty minutes' notice is one of those universally bemusing matters that best remain uninvestigated. Quite simply, there are people who are natural procurers. Or have good rowboat contacts. Gustave is one.

It mattered not to him that I had telephoned before 8 a.m. in a state of alarm and briefly explained my problem. His New Year's Eve party, populated as I had assumed with several dozen women in Joan of Arc fancy dress, was still bubbling along when I rang. It was not raging, as younger folk say, but there were several guests sitting languorously around Gustave's home, having coffee and freshly prepared croissants.

Some of the Joans had taken to Gustave's bed, where he left them in peace to sleep off the effects of his hospitality. Another Joan was snoozing soundly beneath the long dining-room table, and yet another behind the couch. Gustave's property was littered with exhausted Joans. Still, he answered my distress call with his usual cultured attentiveness, and before long we were in the little wooden rowboat.

Gustave sits with his back to the bow, pulling on weathered oars. Between us, in the boat's damp and fishy well, there are a silver martini shaker and two glasses wrapped in a white cloth. In Gustave's pocket is a small sachet of green olives.

'You are okay?' he asks, not in the least breathless from the oar pulling.

'Yes,' I say.

'There is nothing to be ashamed of,' he says.

'No.'

'It is a mistake made by the most honourable of men.'

'I suppose.'

'It is a time-honoured *faux pas*.'

'It has never happened to me before.'

'It is the way,' he says, 'when you put yourself out into the world.'

'The way?'

'*Oui.*'

I sit with my head down, listening to the slap of harbour water against the bows of the old boat. In the distance I hear the sounding of air horns and the laughter of party-goers. Someone, somewhere, smashes a bottle.

Gustave keeps rowing.

'You are not a failure,' he says.

'Thank you, Gustave.'

'You know, there was a saying in my village. If you stray too far from the waterwheel, you get dizzy with thirst.'

'I thought you were born in Paris.'

'Who is born in Paris? We are all born in villages.'

'You were born in a village with a waterwheel?'

'You are missing the point. At some stage, *oui*, there must have been a waterwheel.'

'I'm thirsty now.'

'Pour us a drink.'

As he rows methodically and with surprising power and efficiency, I unwrap the two glasses and fill them from the chilled martini shaker. He passes me the olives without missing a beat in his rowing, and I drop one carefully into each drink. Gustave rests the oars, and we float in the middle of Sydney Harbour.

'To you,' says Gustave, raising his glass.

'Happy New Year, Gustave.'

'Yes, to another year.'

We sip the martinis and I feel the gin working its way through my tired and humiliated body. I am both electrified and depressed by the drink, as fine as it is.

'Tell me again,' he says.

'Tell you what?' I know what he wants but I am reticent.

'The story of last night. Of this woman, Eve.'

I wince at the sound of her name. And that it comes from

the mouth of such a fine and respectable figure as Gustave. I feel I have soiled Gustave by telling him of Eve.

'I don't know where to start.'

'You both got off the boat,' says Gustave, looking at me keenly across the top of his martini glass. 'You walked into Double Bay.'

'Yes, yes, into Double Bay.'

'Where she asked you up to her hotel room for a drink.'

'For a drink, yes.' My eyes are closed now. I pinch the slender stem of the martini glass between my fingers.

'You went up into the room.'

'Yes, Gustave. Yes. I went up to the room. I thought nothing of it.'

'Of course not,' says Gustave, reassuring me. 'As men, we have occasion to walk into hotel rooms, hmm?'

'Yes, that's right. As men we do.'

'Who hasn't walked into a stranger's hotel room?' says Gustave. I open my eyes and look at him briefly. He smiles with one corner of his mouth. 'Into the web, hmm?'

'Yes, the web.'

Gustave finishes the martini and smacks his lips. We have drifted closer, oars up, to Goat Island, our ultimate destination. Gustave clasps his hands and gives me his full attention.

'So then, she opens the champagne for you both, yes? You are sitting on the balcony of her hotel room, having the champagne.'

'That's right.'

'She is pretty, no? This Eve. You have been together all night and there is the attraction.'

'Yes,' I say weakly. 'The attraction.'

'You are a man looking for love, eh? It is not easy, finding the love these days.'

'No, it's not, Gustave.'

'No, it's not, *mon ami*. Most definitely not. The love, it is as scarce as a good martini, no?' With this he flicks my arm with his left hand. I smile at this companionship.

'We are on the balcony,' I continue.

'*Oui.*'

'And we finish our champagne.'

'*Oui, oui.*'

I drain my drink at this point and Gustave immediately refills it. I can feel the martini chilling the glass again. He drops a second olive into the glass. Seagulls cry at us overhead. We inch quietly towards Goat Island.

'She stands and takes me by the hand.'

'Ah yes,' says Gustave. 'The moment of the taking of the hand. It is, *mon ami*, my favourite moment.'

'I have often thought the same,' I say, thinking of my early years with Margaret. And the hand-playing with the young Virginie.

'The taking of the hand, with the lights of the world beyond the balcony of a hotel. Oh, *oui*. Beautiful. Beautiful.'

I can sense Gustave trying to say to me that this has happened to all men. That the moment of the taking of the hand is a confusing one, a moment when time holds its breath and anything can happen. Gustave says, without saying it, that all men have been there. And fallen.

'So she led me inside.'

'Into the hotel room.'

'And she walked me over to the bed.'

'Yes, yes. The bed. We are on the bed.'

I swallow hard. I twirl the martini glass with my finger-tips. I watch the glass go round, and the two olives, large and green and settled in the base of the glass, remain in their exact positions as the martini and the glass and the whole world spin round them.

'I can't continue,' I say.

'You must.'

'It is too embarrassing.'

'It is the embarrassment that makes us what we are.'

'It is?'

'To stare down the folly, *mon ami*. To say we are human. That is the key.'

'She seemed so beautiful.'

'Good,' says Gustave. 'Go on. She was beautiful. Yes. That was obvious, to any man.'

'We kissed, again and again.'

'Good, good.'

'She removed my clothes, right there, on the end of the bed.'

'Very good.'

'The lights were off, but the room . . . you could see things in the light through the open doors to the balcony.'

'Of course.'

'And I began to disrobe her, Gustave.'

'Naturally, yes, as you would, *mon ami*, in this situation. No? *Oui*. Proceed.'

'And then . . .'

'Yes.'

'It was then . . .'

'You must stare down the folly.'

'It was then I realised Eve was not Eve at all. Not Eve, Gustave. No Eve. There was no Eve. Eve, Eve was . . .'

'*Oui*, say it *mon ami*.'

'. . . a man. Eve was a man.'

'Good,' says Gustave. 'Finish your drink and allow me to row. We will be there in five minutes.'

I swallow the remains of the martini and stare at the two moist and perfect green olives resting side by side in the base of the glass.

TWENTY-FIVE

That Which Cannot be Hunted

I AM no prude.

During my lengthy discourse with my psychiatrist over the past months, never once has he labelled me prudish. Indeed, I have recounted certain scenes of a sexual nature to him and noticed a distinct wiggling of *his* toes inside those perennial white tennis socks he wears with his suit.

'You are wiggling again,' I said at a session shortly before the end of the millennium.

'The wiggling,' he said, reclining on his own couch, parallel to mine, with his eyes closed, 'is an external, non-verbal expression of extreme interest in the subject matter under discussion.'

'You are not uncomfortable?'

'I'm very comfortable, thank you.'

'With the topic at hand?'

'My dear fellow, I've heard many things in this room. You cannot shock me.'

'You are unshockable?'

'I am not saying that. My point is, you would have to go a long way to present me with something so outstandingly fresh that it would rattle me.'

'You are very confident of this?'

'Damn tootin'.'

I have become increasingly annoyed by his Midwest American affectations. I have no idea where someone would pick up 'damn tootin'.

'Sexual relations with animals?'

'Heard it more times than you've had hot breakfasts.'

'Oedipus complexes?'

'Par for the course,' he said.

'Foot fetish?'

'Please. Something a little more challenging.'

'You are unoffendable?'

'If I were to make a film on psychiatry and myself, I would call it *The Unoffendables*.'

'You know,' I said, 'your white socks look utterly ridiculous with those dark suits of yours.'

I have never felt he was a particularly insightful psychiatrist, anyway. And in a way I blame him for the monstrous fracas that occurred with Eve on and after the New Year's harbour cruise. (I should have seen something unusual arising from a party attended by 200 therapists.) What a meal my white-socked friend would make out of the story if he learned I had been lured into a hotel room by a man in a particularly fetching frock.

Instead, and as always, Gustave is there to pick up the

pieces in this period in my life when there are more pieces than a whole.

'I am in pieces,' I say to Gustave as he rows towards Goat Island on this shameful morning after the encounter with Eve.

'*Oui*,' he says.

'I want to be whole,' I say.

'*Pardon*?' he replies, his eyebrows raised.

'Nothing,' I say, and we continue on.

I have not divulged to Gustave why I want to return to Goat Island, but I do not have to. He understands. It is the place where I first made love to Margaret. The French, I have learned, accept these superstitious and often irrational matters of the heart.

On my recent farce in France, where I had planned to settle in the little port town of Collioure and become mayor, Virginie had, following a lengthy discussion about the supernatural, slipped me a card with a name and phone number on it. She urged me to telephone the number and make an appointment.

The gentleman in question was a Monsieur Blanc. A strange name, I conceded, for someone who could predict the future. But to Monsieur Blanc's I proceeded early one morning. He lived in the old part of Dijon, in a tiny one-bedroom apartment that had probably once been someone's water closet.

After the initial pleasantries in broken English, he lured me into his bedroom, which was occupied entirely by a giant carved wooden bed. By entirely, I mean it was actually impossible to walk around the bed itself due to lack of leg room. I had no idea how he had lodged the bed there, or if the apartment itself had perhaps come after the bed.

Over on his substantial windowsill was his computer, and we clambered across his embroidered-farm-scene coverlet to inspect the screen.

In short, Monsieur Blanc had devised a scheme whereby he could predict your future from how you coloured in a banded pyramid, bar after bar, from base to pinnacle.

Some people, he explained with difficulty, would simply say they wanted the entire pyramid black or white, or half black, half grey. Others selected different colours for each bar, giving the pyramid a rather carnival effect. It was up to the individual.

Once the colours were keyed in, Monsieur Blanc pressed a sequence of numbers and your future was printed out. He had millions of combinations, or so he said, and a 97 per cent accuracy rate.

I cannot recall the colours I selected, owing to my mental discomfort at sitting on Monsieur Blanc's embroidered-farm-scene coverlet.

It was only while returning to Australia in the plane that I found his crumpled predictions folded in my hand luggage and read them in full.

I would, he said, find comfort in the past. I would correct old wrongs. I would emerge refreshed and vital. I would also one day own a truffle farm. I guess that fell into his 3 per cent inaccuracy range.

Gustave rows steadily towards Goat Island. He has

formidable arms. Perhaps it is an unexpected by-product of cutting so many perfect limes.

'We are almost there,' he says.

'I could do with another martini.'

'You must always visit the past with a clear head.'

'Why is that?'

'Because returning to anything has with it, as you say, the emotional baggage.'

'You're right, Gustave.'

'You must know it is not always successful, the returning.'

'Of course.'

'It is said it can never be done. Pfffttt! I have done it myself.'

'Really?'

'*Mais oui.*'

'I cannot imagine you ever being as frayed as I am.'

'It was not a fraying – is that the word? – it was for pleasure, my friend.'

'You can return successfully with pleasure?'

'Sometimes yes, it is possible. Pleasure is a very welcoming old friend.'

'I have lost that friend.'

'That friend is always around the corner.'

'I am pleasureless.'

'You have shut yourself down. In this way, the pleasure, she cannot find you.'

I shudder at the thought of Eve in the darkened hotel room.

We arrive, finally, at the little jetty on Goat Island and

Gustave expertly lashes the rowboat to a pylon and helps me ashore. I have yet to regain my land legs, and I wobble acutely as we walk around the island.

We stroll in silence until I find the place where Margaret and I picnicked and made love all those years ago. There Gustave and I sit in the shade of the trees.

We look out at the harbour without speaking, wearing the expression that a man wears when he is either lost in thought and staring out at a stretch of water, or is accompanying a man lost in thought who is staring out at a stretch of water.

'It is difficult,' I say, eventually.

'*Pardon*? What is difficult?'

'Life.'

'*Oui.*'

'If you question it, it can give you nothing but grief.'

'*Oui.*'

'And if you don't, it can be happy yet meaningless.'

'*Oui.*'

'And what is love in the twenty-first century? Because that is where we are, Gustave, make no mistake about that. We are firmly in the twenty-first century. That is where we are.'

'*Oui.*'

'You look for dialogue, yet nobody wants to talk about anything meaningful. You are interesting if you live in a mansion on the harbour, but not if you're in a one-bedroom red-brick flat. You want companionship, but you still have to be free to come and go as you please, to do what you have to do, scale ladders, stab backs, walk all over others. You can be married and live in separate countries.'

'*Oui*. It is, as you say, perplexing.'

'Nothing's ever enough. There's always a better job. A better partner. A better opportunity for a better life. By the time you've inspected all the better, greener grass, you've run out of life.'

'*Oui*. It is not so good, this running out of life.'

'I am facing the wall, Gustave. I have nowhere left to turn.'

I stare out at the harbour.

'*Mon ami*,' he says, 'to enjoy the life, in the moment, you cannot try and capture it, you know, in the hands. It will always escape you if you hunt it. It is the thing that cannot be hunted.'

'I don't understand.'

'To attain it, you must let go of everything. *Oui*. The past and the future. Let them drift away. Then you must give yourself over to the moment. Let the moment take over. Am I clear?'

'Surrender to the moment.'

'*Oui*. If you surrender to enough moments, one after the other, *voilà*, *mon ami*, you have a life that is, as they say, worth living.'

We sit in silence for several minutes following Gustave's revelations. Then it comes to me. I will find Margaret, and settle things with finality. I will bring my heart to some sort of peace, and then surrender to as many moments as I can.

I turn to Gustave, and do something I have never done before. I kiss him on both cheeks.

'It is a kiss in the European manner, of course,' I say, smiling.

'Pfffttt!' says Gustave. 'Of course.'

TWENTY-SIX

Life Raft of the Goose

SITTING on Goat Island and contemplating life and love, I wish Gustave had brought a larger martini shaker.

I have always found that things make perfect sense after the third martini. The first is just a primer. A concrete apron to the suburban house of clear thought and understanding.

It's the second, oh, the second, where things begin to come together. Where freshly minted planets form in the infinite universe of the cranium.

The infinite universe of the cranium? I wish I had a coaster and pencil to jot that down.

I cannot even tell Gustave, as he has wandered off to explore the island and leave me in 'the thoughts of the solitary man, *naturellement*'.

He has, in fact, gone to see if Sydney Harbour any longer sustains shellfish, being the student of shellfish that he is, and to wander amongst the rocks that litter the island's periphery.

As for the martini, a second without a third is like having

only seven or so commandments, which cannot have the historic ring of ten. It is incomplete. Unimaginable. I don't know how Gustave can have been so absent minded as to leave me high and dry, so to speak.

How awful it is when a human being loses love, I think. How sadly we trudge back to landscapes of previous happiness and pick through them like apprentice archaeologists for any remnants, any skerricks at all of that past civilisation, that magnificent semblance of ordered disorder known as being in love.

I begin to think coming back to Goat Island has been a mistake. What was left of Margaret but some nettles in my backside, a whiff of oil from across the harbour, an empty martini shaker and a missing barman scavenging for old oyster shells?

As my psychiatrist had instructed once upon a time, I begin to collate a mental list of what has happened to me in the time since Margaret and I went our separate ways.

I have never been one for lists. I know people who make lists of their lists. I once featured in a friend's 'To Do' list as: 'Persuade Wilson to start making lists.' This puzzled me for months. I felt entangled in some bizarre, as yet unfinished Einsteinian equation, lassoed into the world of lists.

But I attempt the mental list all the same. I recall my initial Off the Rails period, and the endless tedium of encounters with well-meaning women. Only now that I am Back On the Rails do I realise that it was, in fact, I who had been endlessly tedious: left floundering in Gold Coast hotel swimming pools, chased trouserless through city streets, wooed women who were really men who wanted to be women wooed by other men who thought they were women.

And all the while there was Margaret, the former base martini of my life.

Where is she? What will she be doing now? I look towards the city and know that she is in there, somewhere, getting on with her life.

I have always marvelled at how well women get on with their lives. How they manage to maintain tack in a forwardly direction, weather the storm, get through to the other side of the squall.

But what to do? I have been to countless hours of therapy, gone bush, discovered my father had dated more women in a month than I had in a year, wandered around France and very nearly become mayor of the small yet picturesque fishing village of Collioure, aged immeasurably, and accidentally grasped a man's genitals on the first day of the new millennium.

I am beginning to frighten myself.

'Gustave!' I shout into the wind, and miraculously he appears, his pockets filled with foul samples of harbour detritus.

'*Oui*?'

'What on earth do you have there?'

'It is for a friend. She makes – what do you call? – the art, the assemblages.'

'Out of fish heads and bug shells?'

'*Mais oui.* She believes that the art must come from the life.'

I have no time to discuss still-life theories with Gustave.

'Gustave, are you a list keeper by any chance?'

'Lists?'

'Yes. Do you write lists to help organise your life?'

'*Mon ami*, the list is the life raft of the goose.'

I am so astounded by this that I am unable to speak for several seconds. I feel the universe has opened a fraction and delivered to Gustave something so profound that it could, potentially, change the world as we know it.

'May I have that? The list is the life raft of the goose.'

'Of course. What am I going to do with it?'

I think, for a moment, that Gustave is perhaps in the wrong job. That he should be penning words of wisdom for the bottoms of calendar pages.

'Gustave, I want to run something by you.'

'Of course.'

'I'm thinking I should contact Margaret again.'

'Margaret?' he asks cautiously.

'Yes, Margaret. My estranged wife.'

He fiddles with a dry oyster shell for a moment.

'So you are saying, if I am not mistaken, that you wish to do the – how do you say in Australia? – track back.'

'Backtrack.'

'Backtrack? It cannot be.'

'No, Gustave, no. Are you trying to say I want to back-track in my life?'

'Backtrack. Are you positive?'

'I'm asking you if this is what you mean, Gustave.'

'The backtrack. It sounds very strange, *mon ami*.'

'Gustave, I'm saying I want to see Margaret again.'

He turns the oyster shell over and over and his forehead creases with concentration.

'You know what this going back entails, *oui*?'

'I think so.'

'As we have discussed, it is said one can never go back. This is, how the English soccer pig would say, bollocks.'

'Did you say bollocks?'

'*Oui*. Bollocks. I have just learned the meaning of the bollocks. I like the sound – yes? – even if it is from the English soccer pig.'

'Why is it bollocks?'

'You can always go back, yes. Look at Monsieur Proust.'

'Now he should have got out more.'

'*Mais oui*!' says Gustave, snorting.

'So is it a good idea? To seek out Margaret again?'

'It can be good or bad. Going back, you can never know what you will find. You may have gone back many times in your head, but to actually go back – it can be a journey fraught with peril.'

'Really?'

'To go back, *mon ami*, takes a greater warrior than one who goes forward.'

'I'm not looking for a fight, Gustave.'

'Then what are you looking for? It is never the same, you know this.'

'It might be close.'

'Even if it is close, on getting there what if you do not like what you find?'

'Do people change that much, Gustave?'

'Physically, over time. Mentally, maybe overnight. Your Margaret, she may be sailing different waters now. You cannot be together if you're on different seas.'

As we row back to the mainland, I am convinced of two things. Firstly, I will take the risk and track down Margaret and see if anything can be salvaged.

Secondly, I will get Gustave an appointment to see the general manager of a greeting card and calendar company.

You cannot be together if you're on different seas. That is far too good to waste on me.

TWENTY-SEVEN

The Dream of the Duck

MY new psychiatrist has strongly advised me to expunge my obsession with F. Scott Fitzgerald's *The Great Gatsby*.

'Why do I get the feeling,' I said to him at our first session, 'that I'm going to pay you extraordinary amounts of money each week just so you can use words like "expunge".'

'That's a trifle unreasonable.'

'You see?' I continued. 'There it is again. With "trifle". Who uses "trifle" these days?'

'I heard it uttered only yesterday.'

'"Uttered" – there's another. You are practising your words on me. I am your verbal driving range.'

'You're overreacting,' he said sternly. 'A tad.'

I foreshortened the session. I actually used the word 'foreshortened'. I could see my therapist was jealous of my having pipped him on 'foreshortened'.

The Gatsby obsession, however, is real. I cannot count the number of times I have read the novel.

How I dreamed, when I was younger and more vulnerable,

of being Nick Carraway. How I wished I had graduated from New Haven and moved to West Egg. And how I longed for a girlfriend who was a golf champion named Jordan.

All that champagne, the parties, the flappers. I fantasise about it to Gustave as I luxuriate in a gin, lime and tonic at the Lime Bar.

'*Pardon*?' he asks.

'Flappers.'

'Flappers? Like with the seals, flappers?'

'No, flappers. It's a term from the Jazz Age, Gustave. For young, attractive, devil-may-care women.'

'That is flappers?'

'That is flappers.'

'But, *monsieur*,' he says with a snort, 'I have heard it called many things, but not flappers.'

'Perhaps there is no equivalent of flappers in French.'

'Most certainly not, *monsieur*. I would not be saying the flappers out loud if I were you.'

'It is from my favourite book, *The Great Gatsby*, Gustave.'

'*Oui*. I have heard of this book. It is about this American Dream *merde*, yes?'

'American Dream. Well, yes, I would say that's probably correct, Gustave.'

He lets off one of his most succinct French pfffttt gunshots.

'American Dream,' he says, shaking his head. 'I would say, *monsieur*, that it would be a very short dream.'

'Now don't be like that, Gustave.'

'I, too, have an American Dream. It is a world without Americans.'

'That's a trifle unreasonable,' I say automatically. I have been infected, somehow, with my new psychiatrist's strange word-utterance disease. 'What about Gatsby?'

'Who is this Gatsby, hmm?'

'A man who believed you could repeat the past.'

'Ahh. Yes. I can see now why you like this Gatsby. It is because of the strange wife, *oui*? Margaret.'

'Estranged.'

'*Ah oui*.'

'You know, Gustave, when I was young I wanted to be Nick Carraway. I *was* Nick Carraway. Young, ambitious, observing the world.'

'Nick . . .'

'Carraway. And now, as I get older, I have become Gatsby. That is the beauty of the book, Gustave. It is why I never tire of reading it. You grow into the characters.'

'It sounds very complicated, *monsieur*.'

'It is life, Gustave.'

'And it is closing time, *monsieur*.'

I stroll along Darling Street, imagining I am heading home to my small cottage in West Egg, and continue down to the ferry wharf.

There, standing alone on the end of the jetty, facing the harbour and the city, I look for the wink of Daisy's green light over in the direction of Milsons Point. I stand with hands in pockets for a long time, gazing wistfully across the Sound.

'Can't repeat the past?' I say to myself incredulously. 'Why of course you can.'

I go home to my flat – which is probably as big as Gatsby's walk-in wardrobe – reread the novel from start to finish with a bottle of brandy for company, and decide to start my search for Margaret.

But in the light of the next day I lose my nerve. That night I retreat to the Lime Bar for solace and encouragement.

'Monsieur Gatsby, what can I get for you?' says Gustave.

I occasionally loathe his sanctimonious Frenchness.

'A flapper on the rocks.'

'Will that be in a tall or short glass?'

'Better make it tall.'

He produces an exquisite gin, lime and tonic, and sits and talks during the lulls.

'You have the face of the sad sack.'

'I want to repeat the past, Gustave, but I have lost the nerve.'

'The nerve must not be lost. The nerve is what gives us the nerve.'

'I won't ask you to repeat that.'

'*Mon ami*, the life is very short. I do not need to tell you this. If you were French this would not be troubling you. What a pity it is that you cannot be French.'

'No, it is a little late for me to be French.'

'It is a shame that more people can't be French.'

'I would like to be French when it suited me,' I say. 'In moments like this.'

'Ah, you wish to turn your Frenchness on and off when you like?'

'Yes, Gustave, yes. I would like to possess itinerant Frenchness.'

Gustave smiles, shakes his head slowly and tsks with the clicking clarity of a summer cicada. 'You are not alone. Millions have mourned before you.'

'It's a damn shame, Gustave. But I must be realistic.'

'This is good,' he says. 'If you cannot be French, be realistic. Go and find your Margaret and bugger off the consequences.'

'Bugger off the consequences?'

'It is my new Australian phrase.'

'I see.'

'What is the worst thing that can happen to you? Hmm? She has another man. So? This is what happens in the life. The man meets the woman. It cannot kill you.'

'It could try. Think of Gatsby.'

'He is the American with the Dream?'

'Yes.'

'Then he's got big problems.'

'Well, he lived life, even if he was shot,' I say, staring into the coloured spirit bottles behind the bar.

'Then go and live life like your Gatsby,' says Gustave. 'Just be careful of the guns, *mon ami*.'

'Yes, Gustave. Always be careful of the guns.'

'The gun is for the duck. Not for *monsieur*.'

'The gun and the duck. How well they go together.'

'Do you think the duck has the dream?'

'Do I think ducks dream?'

'*Non*. Is there a Duck Dream, like there is an American Dream?'

'It is a very esoteric question, Gustave.'

'Is the duck born with the dream of the gun?'

Gustave always has the ability to floor me with his verbal dexterity.

'I would like to think so. For the sake of the duck.'

'Always be prepared, *mon ami*. That is the Duck Dream. Always be prepared.'

'I promise I will, Gustave. I promise.'

And that is when Margaret walks into the bar.

TWENTY-EIGHT

A Woman Called Home

WHEN I see Margaret I am rendered frozen. I have often envisaged the day when we would bump into each other again, and gone over my reaction a thousand times.

But now that it is upon me, now that it is happening, my circuitry completely fails.

She is with a man much older than herself and they do not, to my eye, appear close.

It is a strange thing to watch from a distance a former companion go through the mechanics of ordinary living – the taking of a drink, the discussion, the hand and face gestures, the crossing of the legs at the ankle, the circular motions made by a foot beneath the table.

I had always thought I would be jealous seeing her not just with another man, but in the world itself. A world without me.

But I observe her with a surprising warmth. I see with great clarity the many attractive attributes she possesses that had, over the duration of our marriage, disappeared from my notice. The way she plays with a tendril of hair on the right side of her face, the way her eyebrows arch and her eyes widen when she finds something particularly funny. The sensual repose of her long-fingered hands.

Her companion seems to vanish, as does everyone else in the bar, and it is just Margaret, and dozens of our shared moments, triggered in my memory by the way she holds her glass and shifts in her chair.

Noticing me at the end of the bar, she stops talking. She touches her companion on the shoulder, and comes towards me.

She moves through the crowd as if in slow motion. And the closer she gets to me the younger she looks. She goes from mid-forties, to mid-thirties, to the girl I had first played canasta with, in the space of 10 metres. Here is the epicentre of my love. Five metres away. Three. Two.

I stare, my mouth agape. I could swear she has just winked at Gustave.

Then she is leaning towards me and whispering in my ear, 'Are you ready for your life now?'

I do not know what she means. Yet I know exactly what she is asking. This is the question that has echoed inside me for too long.

'Yes,' I say.

And she gently clasps my upper arm and kisses me on the mouth.

I let my tumbler slip from my fingers onto the coaster. I feel those beautiful, familiar lips against mine and close my eyes. I smell citrus. The essence of Margaret.

And I vanish, entirely, into her. In a split second, and after thousands of tired hours, I have come home.

When finally I open my eyes she is gone, except for her business card on the silver top of the bar.

This night I break my record: I ask Gustave for twelve and a half limes.

TWENTY-NINE

In the Light of the Flaming Ox

'HER business card,' I say indignantly to Gustave. 'I am, in short, flummoxed.'

'Flamed ox?' asks Gustave, bemused.

'Flummoxed, Gustave, flummoxed. Bamboozled.'

'What is this, using the silly words from the playground? Why can't you speak in English, hmm?'

'I beg your pardon,' I say, turning Margaret's card over in my hands.

'You are so easily off-railed, my friend.'

'Did you say off-railed?'

'What else? You don't understand English because your wife gives you her business card?'

'I . . .'

'What did you expect her to give you, hmm? A pair of her nylons? You are a very silly man.'

'But it's so formal, Gustave. After the things we shared together.'

'The things we shared together,' he snorts. 'Why don't

you write her a long letter and sprinkle it with the water of the *toilette*, hmm? You silly schoolboy. Pfffttt!'

I know Gustave is frustrated when he lets off an unexpected pfffttt.

'I am merely saying, Gustave, that this woman and myself shared a life together once upon a time.'

'*Mon Dieu*! Once upon a time. For years now I have been trying to bring you to some . . . some . . . some level of the civilised. The sophistication. But for what? You live in a world – what is the word? – side by side to this one.'

'Parallel.'

'In the parallel world. What can I say any longer? Hmm?'

He slices the nipple from a lemon and it shoots off the bar and rolls under a stool.

I try to shore up my case.

'Just look at this, Gustave. Here, look at her business card. Look. I feel I should make an appointment to see her. I feel . . .'

'Why do you think she gave it to you, you silly man?'

'Well, I . . .'

'It is simple, no? She wants you – and I don't know why, oh my goodness I don't know why – to telephone her. To make contact. What did you expect?' he repeats. 'Her lipstick print on a napkin?'

'Actually . . .'

'Oh *monsieur*. When you have finished at the *lycée* please come back and we can talk.'

'I never imagined it happening this way. It's been a long time, Gustave. What would I say? What would I do?' I am trying to ignore Margaret's question to me. And my answer. Was I really ready for my life? Ever?

Gustave puts down his knife and wipes his hands.

'Let me ask you, *monsieur*. Has a woman ever given you her business card?'

'Of course.'

'*Oui*. Why did she do that? To start a business with you? To make sure she secures those orders for your little Eiffel Towers? Hmm?'

'Er . . .'

'Telephone your past wife, hmm? Say you would like to have luncheon. Or a dinner, perhaps. Yes, a dinner in a dark restaurant for you, so you can cry your schoolboy tears without so many noticing. Is it so hard for you? I am, of course, not telling you what to do.'

'I have not been out for dinner with a woman, one on one, since my trip to France.'

'Pfffttt! That was not dinner with a woman, *monsieur*, if what you tell me is correct. With the grilled meats and the little girl with the soil of the field under her fingernails. What a little way you have come after all.'

'I'm out of practice. Out of dinner practice.'

Gustave tsks and shakes his head. 'Do you want me to dress up in the frock for you to have your practice? Pfffttt! It is the ride of the bicycle.'

'For you. The French are always riding bicycles.'

'I will arrange for your practice, *mon ami*. Leave it to me.'

'Really?'

'*Oui, oui*.'

'I'm excited.'

'I will have the little driver's learner plate made up.'

'What for?'

'For your backside, *monsieur*.' His cloth squeaks as he dries a glass with his usual French vigour. 'We cannot have the learner driver running around, as you say, nilly willy. Hmm?'

THIRTY

In the Brasserie des Affaires

THE restaurant where I am to be a learner diner before my reunion with Margaret is not, in fact, called the Brasserie des Affaires. Not in public quarters at least. That is its code name.

And it is not an entirely fashionable establishment, tucked away as it is in the backstreets of East Sydney. For those unaware of its peculiar double life, it is simply Ernie's Eatery.

From the street it would not attract you. There is no wide window at the front through which diners can observe street life between dishes. There is a window, yes, but it is perennially shuttered.

The front door is of a heavy and weathered wood. There are insets of frosted amber glass. You can often see light from the restaurant through the amber glass, but that is all. The lights burn well into the early hours of the morning. Ernie's would seem to keep elastic hours.

Inside, the décor is hardly remarkable. Solid wooden tables and chairs, dim lighting, exposed brick walls. The tables are generously sized for two. Four at a table would be a squeeze. Ernie's primarily caters for couples. What it lacks in aesthetics, however, it makes up for in a fine wine list and some of the best French cuisine in the city.

You will not find Ernie's in a phone book or a restaurant guide. And you will never see Brasserie des Affaires written down – anywhere.

Gustave, having long observed me in my loveless angst, has finally decided to let me in on one of the city's greatest secrets: the Brasserie des Affaires. Here I am to practise dining with a woman before my rendezvous with Margaret. If I practise successfully, and Margaret and I resume our life together, all very well. If Margaret and I do not become reconciled, I can resume my quest for love here, at the Brasserie, at a future time convenient to the establishment and my emotional stability. I am unsure who has the longer waiting list in these quarters.

'A restaurant for what?' I ask, incredulous.

'*Mon ami*,' Gustave says, whispering. 'Keep your voice down. It must never be mentioned outside this conversation.'

'It's a French restaurant that caters for —'

'Shhhhh. I will not warn you again or I cannot impart to you what I have to impart.'

'I apologise.'

'If word of this gets out the place is finished, do you understand?'

'I understand.'

'I'm not sure you do. One pair of loosey lips and they are out of business overnight.'

'Did you say loosey lips?'

'You know, loosey. The lips that wag too much.'

'If you knew loosey like I know loosey, Gustave.'

'It is run by a very good friend of mine, *mon ami*. I am risking that friendship by even telling you what I have already told you. It is a very difficult situation for me. But I see you are in need.'

'I am most definitely in need, Gustave.'

'Monsieur Ernie – that also is not his real name, but I must be careful, you can understand – would approve in this case. But everything I tell you must be forgotten immediately.'

'Immediately? I'm still not quite sure what you're talking about.'

'Come closer, *mon ami*, and I will explain one last time.'

'Yes, yes.'

He looks around furtively and then leans over the silver top of the bar.

'This is a place that only caters for people having the affairs or looking for the affairs —'

'Yes?'

'That is all I can say.'

'You mean there's an entire restaurant in East Sydney that just looks after people committing adultery or secretly frolicking?'

'I did not say that specifically, *mon ami*, but you are beginning to understand.'

'A whole restaurant exclusively for cheaters?'

'I do not know this cheaters. What is cheaters?'

'People fooling around with other people.'

'Yes, there is a lot of the fooling around. There is only the fooling around at the Brasserie des Affaires.'

'You're kidding me.'

'Fooling around is no joke, *mon ami*.'

I sit back on my stool to digest Gustave's revelation. It seems so completely insane that it begins to make sense.

'So you can just walk in off the street and fool around?'

'No, no. You can only make a booking and your booking will only be accepted if you say you wish to dine in the Brasserie des Affaires.'

'But it's called Ernie's Eatery, so you say.'

'Yes, *mon ami*, correct. You can never come in off the street, as you say, and ask for a table in Ernie's Eatery. It is always fully booked, even when it's not fully booked. If you understand me.'

'I see. I think.'

'Only by making a reservation for the Brasserie des Affaires are you permitted a table.'

'That is the code?'

'That is the code.'

'How very French, Gustave.'

'Every nationality has its codes.'

'But how many have a code for love, Gustave?'

He smiles. 'Now you are truly beginning to understand, *mon ami*.'

'And illicit love at that.'

He smiles even more broadly.

'In the world of illicit love, *monsieur*, there are the most precious codes of all.'

'Why are you telling me all this, Gustave? What are you trying to say?'

'I am saying there is a place for people who are tired of being loveless. A place where there are other people who are exhausted by the search, the hunt as you call it. There are many people to love, but how do those people get together? It is the French way, *monsieur*, to see that love is given a chance. The Brasserie des Affaires is one such place.'

'You are very kind to me, Gustave.'

'*Oui*.'

'And very French.'

'If you are French it is best to be very French.'

Gustave serves me another gin, lime and tonic and then, using the phone behind the bar, has a hushed but animated discussion before returning to me.

'My friend Ernie says you are most welcome this evening. There has been a cancellation and he says the duck *confit* is particularly fine tonight.'

'But what am I to do there?' I ask, moderately alarmed. 'I'm not looking for an affair. I'm supposed to be in training for Margaret. How can I go to a brasserie that's only interested in people wanting affairs?'

'You will see, *mon ami*. They will look after you.'

He writes down the address and phone number on a slip of paper.

'Take this,' he says, sliding the paper across the bar, under his hand, 'and eat it once you have given the taxi man the address.'

'Eat it?'

'*Oui.*'

'I'm not in the French resistance, Gustave.'

'This is not the making of fun time, *monsieur*. Love is war. The French have always understood that.'

'I won't argue.'

So it is that I take a cab to East Sydney and press the intercom button of Ernie's Eatery.

'Yes?' says a voice.

'The Mareeba limes are the juiciest,' I say in code, just as I have rehearsed with Gustave.

And the door buzzes in welcome. As I step into the restaurant I think, for no reason but the obvious, of Harry Lime in *The Third Man*. If I were to be greeted with zither music, I would not be surprised.

Instead, I am virtually embraced by the beaming and diminutive maître d' who, steering me with a little hand in the small of my back, escorts me to the lounge bar at the rear of the restaurant.

The barman instantly serves me a dish of fresh limes, a tumbler of gin and a chilled crystal jug of tonic water. The phone behind the bar rings. I pour my drink and look around the long, dimly lit room. I clearly hear the barman whisper, '*Oui*, he has arrived.'

Men and women chat convivially in the bar booths nearby. I take several sips, unsure of what will happen next.

Just as I drain my gin and tonic, the little maître d' appears at my side.

'Your table is ready, *monsieur*,' he says.

'Thank you, Jeeves,' I say. I have no idea why I call him

Jeeves, but attribute it to my ebullient state, to a reckless-
ness that the Brasserie des Affaires has already instilled in
me. I am here, in the beating heart of adultery, subterfuge,
cryptic notes, coded messages, and creamy limbs against
velvet in the low light.

As I accompany the maître d' I feel very much the naughty
boy, aflutter with expectation, and not a little weak-kneed
and dry in the throat (is it Gustave's note still lodged there?)
at the thought that I am stepping into a new life. Perchance a
step towards Margaret. If not, at least a step.

'He's on his way to his table,' I hear the barman say, and
turning I catch him placing the phone back in its cradle.

'Over here, *monsieur*,' the maître d' says. 'The lady is
waiting.'

The dining room is aglow with tiny islands of light, the
table lamps sketching, or so it seems to me, just the hands
and wrists and arms and shadowed faces of a world of
lovers. You can feel *amour*, thick and perfumed and heady,
flowing around the tables. The maître d', in front of me, all
but disappears, save for his white cuffs and starched collar.

I identify what I think must be my table in the far corner
and the shape of a woman, her hands clasped and her
elbows resting on the table. I still cannot see her face with
any clarity as the maître d' pulls out my high-backed chair.

'*Monsieur*,' he says.

I sit down slowly, and enter the faint plane of light from
the flickering table lamp. And there, across from me, is the
beautiful face, the only face in my life, then and now. It is
Margaret.

She reaches across the table and takes my right hand.

'You're a couple of years late,' she says.

Nervously I press the knuckle of her thumb. I cannot speak.

'I'm reliably told the duck *confit* is very good this evening,' she says.

'Margaret . . .'

She takes my other hand.

'It's all right.'

'I . . .'

She squeezes my hands and looks briefly over my shoulder. Turning my head to follow her gaze, I catch both the jockey maître d' and the barman smiling at the far end of the room.

'As a good friend of ours might say,' Margaret murmurs, 'sometimes the no speaks says everything.'

We laugh then. Laugh two-years'-worth of laughing. I laugh so deeply and completely I have tears in my eyes.

THIRTY-ONE

Hour of the Sidecar

HOW my barman, Gustave, and I have ended up on a week-long vacation in Byron Bay courtesy of a food-warming display cabinet is a long, and at times sad, story.

But, as my Great-aunt Dot always said, life can turn on a sixpence.

'A sex ponce?' Gustave asks as we check into the Beach Hotel.

'Sixpence, sixpence. A small coin.'

'Ah,' he says vacantly, his mind still back at the Lime Bar, and the glass-and-chrome food warmer that has precipitated this dramatic turn in his life.

Once unpacked, we settle instantly on the poolside cabana lounges and order cocktails. Gustave is polite about my Hong Kong Handover '97 swimming trunks. He utters not a peep. Then again, he has reached a crossroads.

'I cannot work there any longer,' he says, staring into the blue pool water.

'Of course not.'

'It is not of my ethics.'

'You must stand by your ethics.'

By chance, we have both arrived at our forks in the road at the same time. I have been presented with a return to Margaret, my wife. With whom I have dined repeatedly since our reunion at the Brasserie des Affaires. With whom I have attended assorted functions – the opera, gallery openings – clean of collar, greying of hair. Margaret who, on my arm, introduces me as her husband. And Gustave? – Gustave has been asked to work alongside a fast-food-warming cabinet. Both are weighty matters.

In its bid to resuscitate a flagging clientele, and despite Gustave's five-star service as a barman, management of the Lime Bar has decided, without consulting staff, to downsize operations as a place of sophisticated atmosphere and upsize operations as a place of beer-barn ambience. It has insulted Gustave's sensibilities, as a Frenchman and a human being.

'I will not continue service in the presence of the pies,' he says.

'It is a slap in the face,' I retort. 'A wallop across both cheeks with a leather glove.'

'Not to mention these – what you call? – the rolls of the sausage. Pfffttt!'

'It is tantamount to a duel,' I continue, warming to my own French fantasies. 'It is pistols at twenty paces.'

Gustave correctly ignores me.

'It is tasteless *merde*.'

'Absolute *merde*, excuse my French.'

It is a rare occasion that I act as counsellor to Gustave. Which is probably a very good thing indeed.

I push on in my new role. I tell him that a sea change is not bad. I tell him that most Australians had been left floundering for decades before the phrase 'sea change' was introduced into the lexicon, courtesy of a television serial. I tell him that this is the way most social change occurs in Australia. That it has to be seen on television first for any form of validation. That it is only real to Australians if it is test driven on the box.

'Sea change,' he muses.

'*Oui*,' I naturally answer.

'Let us walk,' he says. 'It is good for the thinking.'

So, like two pensive gents who perhaps write poetry and collect stamps in their spare time, we stroll the boulevards of Byron Bay at dusk, even though there are no boulevards to speak of, and mull over our respective lives.

Mull, it proves, is entirely appropriate. We have not ambled 10 metres down the beach when we encounter the overpowering aroma of marijuana drifting across the cool sand from dozens of groups of youthful and not so youthful locals huddled together at the water's edge.

I feel a little light-headed. Gustave shows no external change in his stoical French demeanour.

As we progress towards the base of the lighthouse I wonder why I never became a hippie in the seventies and wore caftans and lived in a teepee.

Probably because I had missed out on having parents who were part of the sixties revolution. Mine were leftover forties and fifties parents. I was never going to have a name like Sunbeam or Sky. Tie-dye was never going to grace the family wardrobes.

On the walk with Gustave, however, pushing through intermittent clouds of dope smoke, I feel fleetingly that it is still not beyond my reach, this nudity and caftan life. That I could reinvent myself as some sort of tribal elder, claim ancestry with dolphins, grow dreadlocks, sit on crystals for their healing powers, sire limitless golden-haired hydroponic hippie children and become adept at the bongos.

There is, of course, the slow and steady return to Margaret. And Gustave's pie warmer.

'You know,' I say to him later, in a very fine restaurant not far from the hotel, 'maybe it's a sign.'

'A sign?'

'Time to move on.'

'Where is there to move to?'

'Another bar. A grand hotel.'

'You miss my point, *mon ami*. It is the same the world over, this culture of the mono.'

'Culture of the mono?'

'This sameness of the world, *monsieur*.'

'Ah, I see.'

'It was why I left my beloved France. Even there – pfffttt! – the signs are all over.'

'The dumbing down of the human race, Gustave.'

'The dumbing, *oui*.'

We order our Asian-Mediterranean-African-Cajun-style fish dishes and have some more wine. Gustave stares hopelessly at the colourful rooster on the label.

'It is the great cultural axiom,' I say, raising my eyebrows at myself, having never used the word 'axiom' before (have I become my own analyst?).

'*Oui*,' says a dejected Gustave, picking at the rooster.

I do not wish to compound his depression. I remind him of the dolphins we had seen that very afternoon, surfing the waves. And the topless horse-rider cantering along the beach. And the fine Norwegian leather slip-ons he had purchased in a local shoe store.

Nothing cheers him.

He toys with his fish, having found it, finally, beneath a thicket of bamboo shoots and ginger, and maintains his far-away look.

I order another bottle of the roosterish wine. The evening continues to flag.

Then it dawns on me.

'You know, Gustave,' I say, 'there is always the Brasserie des Affaires.'

I do not attempt to lower my voice when speaking of the fabled Brasserie. We are far enough away from Sydney, I think, to converse in an unfettered way about that establishment. Gustave does not chastise me, either.

'Explain, *mon ami*.'

'Perhaps we both need a change. You know, my career as a vendor of souvenirs has not been without its unsatisfying moments.'

How can I tell him the extent of my misery in the trade when he is so immersed in his own problems? Could he comprehend how debasing it is to be a dealer of Uluru butter dishes and Opera House garlic presses? Could he possibly imagine?

'*Oui*,' he says.

'Enter – the Brasserie des Affaires, Gustave.'

'*Oui, oui*. I am not understanding.'

'We could buy it out, you and me. Take it over.'

'Buy it out?'

'Why not? You could run it how you wished. Turn it into something even more unforgettable.'

'The Brasserie?'

'Create an oasis. A place free of the culture of the mono.'

'Free.'

'A place of another time, another era. Where the waiters wear high starched collars. A place of cigarette girls and fringed shades on the little table lamps.'

'On the *petites lampes*, *oui*.'

'A place, Gustave, that celebrates the hour of the Sidecar.'

'The hour of the Sidecar?'

'The Sidecar, Gustave, the Sidecar.' I am, for some inexplicable reason, warming to a strange sort of philosophical notion about this lost cocktail, this drink that epitomised elegance in another age.

'The hour, Gustave, the hour when you disappear into another time, another place. An era in history you belong to. Not the era you have been born into.'

'*Oui, oui*. The place where the heart and the soul have always belonged.'

'There are people,' I say, relishing my new role as worldly

theorist, 'who are clearly born out of their real time. You are one such person, Gustave.'

'And you, *mon ami*, if I may say.'

'You may say, Gustave.'

'Then I am saying.'

'Consider it said,' I say.

'The Brasserie. The Sidecar. *Mon ami*,' he says, raising his empty glass and smiling.

'*Garçon!*' I shout. 'More rooster, if we may.'

THIRTY-TWO

Love Story in a Matchbook

I HAVE received a letter from my mother telling me she has finally left my father and has run away with the leader of an amateur chamber ensemble in Kangaroo Valley.

She informs me they met at a rural market, where he was displaying an array of fruits and vegetables from his valley farm. She says his asparagus were particularly firm, and that he owes his success to playing his violin in the fields late at night.

I cannot blame her. My father has been playing in the fields at night for many years.

I call my father on the telephone and he answers it with an almost indecent haste. He sounds old and sad and alone now that he does not have the creeping tendrils of my mother's cigarette smoke in the house.

'Why don't you drop by for dinner?' he asks.

'I will, Father. When would suit you?'

'How about tonight?'

'It's 9 in the evening, Father. And I'm with someone.' I cannot say Margaret's name to him.

'Oh,' he says.

After the call I measure his fractured voice against the sprightliness of my mother's letter and her lyrical descriptions of eddying rock pools, and cockatoos at dawn, and a room full of books, and a stone fireplace, and the gentle notes of a violin travelling perfectly through the dewy stems of asparagus, and her impending seventy-second birthday, and I shake my head in wonder.

'My mother has run off with an asparagus farmer,' I tell Gustave later.

'*Bon*. I am interested in the quality of this lover's asparagus. If it is not too delicate a subject, *mon ami*.'

'Not at all.'

'The break-up of the parents. It is like a death, *non*?'

'They're in their seventies, Gustave.'

'You do not know this, *mon ami*, but my mother also ran off, as you say, with a church organist from Lyon.'

'An organist?'

'*Oui*. It seems it is the music with our mothers. The violin of the chamber, the organ of the church.'

'And your father?'

'He disappeared to a little village you may know from your travels – Collioure – and for many years has just slept and read the books and grown a little garden. He swims every day in the harbour, backward and forward. Pfffttt. It is very un-French, *mon ami*.'

I am speechless. I recall the elderly man freestyling in

the harbour before I was booted out of that pretty southern village by the toe of Christ.

'He was the intellectual. The philosopher. And he disappears to swim every day in silence. This is what the organ did to my father. I cannot listen to the music of the organ.'

I become concerned about my own father.

I discover he has not played golf in three weeks and think it is time to visit him at home. As I turn into our street I see him, at a distance, getting into his car. I follow him. I feel a little soiled and disloyal tracking him, but I need to know what he does now that he has been tossed aside for an asparagus farmer.

He drives all the way out through Mosman, then down into the National Park with its scattering of fibro houses and barbed-wire fences. He parks beneath a stand of gums and, in his shorts and T-shirt and carrying a towel, waddles down a short stretch of road, then disappears into the harbourside lantana.

I stalk him at a safe distance. He takes a track through the lantana, negotiating it cautiously down to a small shady cove. I leave the track and battle through the undergrowth until I find a decent vantage point on the sandstone cliffs that hug the beach.

Moments later I see my father place his towel neatly on the gritty sand and completely disrobe. He stretches briefly, puts his hands on his hips and gazes out to sea, then lies down on his back on the towel and scratches his genitals.

I creep closer to the cliff edge and, looking down, see dozens of men of the same age, all of them nude, sunbaking, resting on their elbows and staring out at the harbour, or strolling along the shore inspecting the water's edge. My father has become an old nudist.

I report this to Gustave.

'*Oui*,' he says, nodding vigorously in complete understanding. 'It is the same with my parents. In the freedom, the mother goes to the music. With the broken heart, the men go to the sea. *Oui. Oui.* It is strange, *non*? Our lives run like the railway tracks.'

I do not understand Gustave's theory. I do not understand why my father has suddenly decided he will see out the rest of his life socialising with old lolling penises. Surely he cannot hope that an attractive young woman, a little bird of brilliant plumage, will flutter onto the sand one day? Is it – as Gustave says – a matter of the primal?

'It is the loss of the malehood, *monsieur*. He is around the penises, *oui*? He is surrounded by the vanishing maleness.'

'You may be right, Gustave.'

'Pfffttt! Without the steady footing of the wife, there can be no naughty infidelities. The men, they fly apart, *mon ami*, like the stick and straw houses of the little pigs, *oui*?'

'Of course, Gustave.'

'We must be very careful of the farmers of the asparagus and the organists when we are in our seventies, *mon ami*,' Gustave says, waggling his finger.

With thoughts of vegetables and my naked father (had it really taken me so many decades to see him naked?) in my head, I feel the need to assemble my numerous jottings on coasters, serviettes and bills of fare from the past few years.

So many coasters. So many musings.

On the inside of a not-so-stylish matchbook from Ernie's Eatery I find I had doodled little caricature heads of myself and Margaret, lassoed both of us with a wobbly heart, and printed over the pale brown flame streaks of long-struck matches 'Love Story in a Matchbook'.

At the end of our reunion meal at the Brasserie des Affaires, the tiny maître d' had ushered Margaret and me through the kitchen and into the restaurant's back alley, where a limousine awaited us. A single, perfect lime on the back seat left me little doubt about who had arranged this most romantic moment.

We were taken to the wharf at Woolloomooloo, then assisted on board a water taxi and delivered, of course, to Goat Island. We giggled like mischievous children, made love under our tree, and talked and kissed and held each other, and I had not even wanted to ask if she had met anyone like a vegetable grower or an organ grinder, and she had asked me nothing as well, and we had kept each other warm against the brisk harbour breeze that whipped and snapped off the water.

Turning the 'Love Story in a Matchbook' about in my hands, I think of this, and of my father still there on the little cove beach, naked on his towel in the dark, and my mother dancing barefoot up and down rows of tilled soil in the moonlight, and Gustave at his farewell party at the Lime Bar.

Gustave understands my absence from the celebrations.

'It is the closing of a book, Gustave. I couldn't face it,' I had told him.

'*D'accord*! Tonight I will cut the limes for the last time, *mon ami*. Then it is over. Pfffttt.'

'We move on.'

'*Oui*. The lime, *mon ami*, has many segments.'

'Of course.'

'The skin is both of the delicate and yet tough, *oui*? As we must be.'

'As we must be, Gustave.'

THIRTY-THREE

Fin (de Siècle)

ONLY after 3 o'clock in the morning do I get to read the tablecloths.

This is my private pleasure. I have not told Gustave, my long-time friend, former cocktail master of the Lime Bar and maître d' here at the Brasserie des Affaires. Not even my wife, Margaret, who after our two years' estrangement returned to my side.

If our restaurant had open front windows you would see me at this hour, after closing time, firstly sitting in my favourite red leather booth at the back of the room, preparing the orders for the next day: a stocky figure, a figure of concentration, his head full of cauliflowers and quails. Then, over a glass of cognac, sitting in the glow of the table lamps, looking out at the landscape that is now my life – thirty wooden tables and their attendant Parisian-café-style chairs. I have had worse geographies.

How I spent years surveying hectares of glow-in-the-dark Hula-hoops and imitation Mickey Mouse children's backpacks, disgorged relentlessly from Chinese factories, is even now a mystery to me. For years I dreamed of Uluru butter dishes and Opera House snow domes and giant black rodent ears eclipsing the sun. My latest psychiatrist assures me those bleak nights are over.

With the cognac finished, I will rise and stroll slowly between the thirty tables and their white paper tablecloths, all of them uniquely besmirched with the journey of steamy and illicit meals. I can tell you about the diners, the lovers, from the canvas of their tablecloths. Sometimes – oh, dear me, yes – they tell me most explicitly about themselves with their graffiti of love.

We do things a little differently at the Brasserie des Affaires. Our name has never been committed to print, as is the tradition. Our dining room only exists in the minds (or loins, in some cases) of our clients. We never advertise. We take no street trade. Our menus and booking sheets are destroyed each evening, the little bonfire personally super-vised by Gustave or me. The head chef, in his first month of employ, varied his public transport route to work to throw off any curious members of the culinary press and nosy fellow chefs. There are no trails to and from the Brasserie des Affaires.

For here, tucked away in this East Sydney backstreet, abutting a factory that deals in imported cane furniture, is a space where men and women can perform, in utter anonymity, the art of the rendezvous. They are all adulterers and mistresses here, dreamers and lovers. They stroke hands and fumble with knees and kiss and cuddle in the wavering lamplight, away from family and spouses and the world. And they doodle on the tablecloths. Lord, how they doodle.

Look. Table Twenty-three. A rather detailed sketch of a tropical beachside bungalow hugged by arching palms. A dream nest for the young lovers. And here, at Seventeen. A swelling heart and arrow of the type drawn for a teenage valentine (rather like 'Love Story in a Matchbook'). Dear, how silly and romantic things can get at the Brasserie. How adults become flirty, flighty children in new love.

We have pomposity, of course. The Shakespearian sonnets printed in capitals to impress. The dreary Keats and Byron. I see a Byron verse and I can tell you an affair is not going to last. But we have some creative clients, and some of their nudes and, how can I say, more graphic depictions of copulating couples have been so good I have – as long as the food splashes are minimal – actually taken them away and had them framed. (It was Margaret's suggestion we provide our diners with a better brand of pencil on arrival, which has, indeed, lifted the quality of the framable doodle.)

We have been running the Brasserie des Affaires for over a year now. It is my most successful business venture. My father, finally, would be proud of me. But I see less and less of him these days, now that he has moved away from Sydney to Anna Bay, where he lives within walking distance of Samurai Beach, the Central Coast's premier nudist spot.

Here at the Brasserie des Affaires we have not had an empty table in seven months (the last was due to a client's unfortunate heart attack prior to dining, which we won't go into). My mother and her new partner – the Kangaroo

Valley asparagus farmer – have dined here twice under assumed names and in disguise. I think they rather enjoyed the ruse. They held hands all evening, even through the main course.

Gustave, of course, is the best unknown maître d' in this city of maître d's. My marriage to Margaret is unshakeable. We had 300 people to the ceremony marking the renewal of our vows. We have a city love nest, a lap pool, and a rowboat in which I take Margaret on long (albeit slow) adventures to the nooks and crannies of the harbour. It is, I like to think, an apt metaphor for our lives now, for the many little coves and bays we are discovering about ourselves in our deep companionship.

I smile quietly at the thought of this. Margaret knew, she has since said, that we would come together again after what Gustave calls my Kite on Fire period. Men are like the snow melt, she says. It takes longer for their river to reach the ocean. I like this, even though I have no idea what it means. It is nice to be with a woman who knows about things such as snow melts. I may take her on a horse-riding trek in the Snowy Mountains.

By 4 in the morning I have gathered the tablecloths, retrieved humorous drawings from them, and turned the rest to ash in a drum in the back alleyway. I stoke the fire with a poker, and on still nights I watch with childlike fascination as the sparks rise in waves to die in the cool night air.

For I am one of those sparks. Bright and fleeting and shooting into the darkness. A trace of life. Or, if you wish to be dictionary pedantic (don't worry, I have gone to the books on this myself), an ignited or fiery particle produced by one hard body striking itself against another.

How do you find love again when everything has been taken away from you? How do you locate that other hard body? And what can you say when what you have been looking for is what you had from the start? In the end, although much is known, it remains a mystery.

I keep these internal ruminations to myself. Heaven forbid that Gustave should know I have turned philosophical. The velocity of his French pffftts is not worth contemplating.

I recall a magazine snippet I read many years ago about the inscription on coffins in some Pacific islands. The inscription, needless to say, pertains to death. But it could as easily apply to the often-disastrous quest for love in a largely loveless world.

Today, I. Tomorrow, you.

How beautifully simple it is. How horrific to think of life and death summarised so deftly with these four words. Is that it? The secret of life? Four words?

Just like the lime, *monsieur*. I can hear Gustave in my head. Four words. Four quarters of the lime. It is as it has always been.

I pfffttt to myself.

Within a few months of Gustave leaving the Lime Bar and my reunion with Margaret, we had bought and refitted the Brasserie des Affaires.

On completion, Gustave slowly surveyed the main dining room with moist eyes and declared, '*Mon ami*, it is – how do you say? – the beautiful dream of this Gustave.' He was, finally, pfffttt-less.

On opening night, at which there were no press, local dignitaries, industry figures or would-be gastronomes – just a handful of tight-lipped philanderers and staff – a photograph was taken in the foyer of the Brasserie's three principal directors: myself, with an arm around Margaret's waist; and standing forever vigilant by the restaurant's rather fetching red velvet greeting banquette and antique rostrum, my Maître d'Hôtel, Gustave.

I have this photograph, framed and sitting on my office desk, as we speak. I notice how happy Margaret and I look. Older, yes. But with the loved one, do we ever lose sight of their youth and beauty, of how they were when we first met and fell in love? It is always there, as we travel together beyond the early stages of lust into the deeper and calmer water of true companionship. (Did I say deeper and calmer water of true companionship? I make a note to myself to be more censorious of liquid analogies.)

Then there is my man, Gustave. How lucky I was to find him so long ago in the Lime Bar. How disastrous things might have been without him. As he often said in those years of repair: '*Monsieur*, we all need the pylon to tether to now and then.'

Most nights I will watch him at work, the way he moves about the tables, draws the room together, facilitates conversation between the nervous and even steers them towards the flickering and hesitant rim of romance's lamplight. (Should I jot that down? Water, now fire. I am doubtful.)

Yes, there are some people who can bring us back in from the dark. But we have to want to be near the flame as well.

'*Bonsoir*,' Gustave says, greeting our guests in his most beautiful French, and trailing a perpetual bouquet of aftershave and his own very unique Gustaveness.

And you can see the women invariably ask him the question en route to their tables.

'*Mais oui*,' he says. 'It is an *eau de toilette*, with an essence of the limes . . . I like to think of it, *madame*, as the fragrance of life.'

They flit after him like moths, and the women (and some of the men, if the truth be known) flutter their eyelids and watch his face as he expertly slides out their chair for them and arranges their napkin on their lap.

'Ah, *merci beaucoup, madame*,' he will say to a question I cannot hear. 'But that I cannot reveal.'

I know the question. And I think I know the answer.

Then Gustave turns his head slightly, a smile at the corner of his mouth, and gives me a delicate and almost imperceptible wink.

Acknowledgements

The author wishes to thank the editor of the *Adelaide Review*, Christopher Pearson, for his encouragement during the *Lime Bar* years. My heartfelt thanks, also, to publisher Clare Forster, who showed enthusiasm from the beginning, and nurtured the project through to the end with typical grace and professionalism. I also salute Bob Sessions and all the hard-working folk at Penguin Books, especially editor Lesley Dunt, whose brilliant and meticulous pencil made the cocktail infinitely smoother.

THE PENGUIN BEST AUSTRALIAN SHORT STORIES

Edited by Mary Lord

This bestselling anthology demonstrates the excellence of the Australian short story from its first flowering in the 1890s through to its exciting maturity in the twentieth century. It includes stories by Peter Carey, Marion Halligan, Marjorie Barnard, Patrick White, Amy Witting and Elizabeth Jolley.

Set in cities, in suburbia and in the outback, Mary Lord's selection of short stories explores the subtleties, the humour and the sadness of human life. For anyone interested in Australian writing and the changing views of Australian writers, this is an essential collection.

THE PENGUIN CENTURY
OF AUSTRALIAN STORIES

Edited by Carmel Bird

This landmark collection brings together the best Australian short stories written in the twentieth century.

From early bush life to contemporary urban existence, *The Penguin Century of Australian Stories* celebrates our finest writers in all their modes: the lively comic fiction of Henry Lawson and Steele Rudd, the distinctive imaginations of Christina Stead and Patrick White, the experimental style of Peter Carey, and the highly lyrical prose of Brenda Walker and James Bradley.

Selected by Carmel Bird, these stories mirror the concerns of Australia's past and present. *The Penguin Century of Australian Stories* will enlighten and entertain for many years to come.